"I hope you didn't leave on my account."

Troy stopped right in front of her. This was the tricky part, the part he didn't like. But it was for Raven's own good. He'd made his decision, and he just needed to follow through. "I'm a big boy, sweetheart. You don't need to mother me."

"I'm not mothering you," she said, frowning as she looked up at him.

"You mother everything. You're the consummate Earth Mother, you know that?" When she looked away, he tipped her chin up. Her eyes went wide open and surprised.

"What are you doing?"

"What do you think I'm doing?"

"I think you're flirting with me."

"Darlin'," he drawled, "if I was flirting with you, you wouldn't be thinking so hard about it. You'd know."

Dear Reader,

I'm very excited about my new stories set in Brody's Crossing, Texas. This fictional small town is north-northwest of Fort Worth, in a cattle- and oil-producing area different than the Hill Country setting for my past seven books, Ranger Springs. I can really identify with this story because like Raven, I married a Texan who considers me a "Yankee," even though I grew up in Kentucky and consider myself rather Southern!

Troy Crawford comes from four generations of a ranching family. When his brother's reserve unit is called to active duty, Troy steps in to run the Rocking C and fix the problems caused by years of stubborn refusal to change with the times. To help him update the ranch, he's expecting a cattle expert from a national organization.

Raven York raises goats, sheep and rabbits on her organic farm in New Hampshire. She's a determined vegetarian who loves animals of all kinds, so when she's sent to Texas to document and restore a heritage garden, she's shocked to find herself on a cattle ranch. She's especially shocked by her attraction to Troy Crawford!

Raven and Troy must work through many differences, but they also discover similarities in their backgrounds and their hopes for the future. Like many of us, they prove that opposites really do attract. I hope you enjoy their story. Look for Clarissa, Ida and the gang in future stories set in Brody's Crossing, Texas. Please visit my Web site, www.victoriachancellor.com, for updates on my upcoming books and previous releases, and have a wonderful summer.

Victoria Chancellor

Temporarily Texan
VICTORIA CHANCELLOR

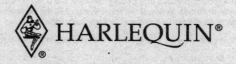

HARLEQUIN®

TORONTO • NEW YORK • LONDON
AMSTERDAM • PARIS • SYDNEY • HAMBURG
STOCKHOLM • ATHENS • TOKYO • MILAN • MADRID
PRAGUE • WARSAW • BUDAPEST • AUCKLAND

ISBN-13: 978-0-373-75176-1
ISBN-10:   0-373-75176-1

TEMPORARILY TEXAN

Copyright © 2007 by Victoria Chancellor Huffstutler.

All rights reserved. Except for use in any review, the reproduction or utilization of this work in whole or in part in any form by any electronic, mechanical or other means, now known or hereafter invented, including xerography, photocopying and recording, or in any information storage or retrieval system, is forbidden without the written permission of the publisher, Harlequin Enterprises Limited, 225 Duncan Mill Road, Don Mills, Ontario M3B 3K9, Canada.

This is a work of fiction. Names, characters, places and incidents are either the product of the author's imagination or are used fictitiously, and any resemblance to actual persons, living or dead, business establishments, events or locales is entirely coincidental.

This edition published by arrangement with Harlequin Books S.A.

® and TM are trademarks of the publisher. Trademarks indicated with ® are registered in the United States Patent and Trademark Office, the Canadian Trade Marks Office and in other countries.

www.eHarlequin.com

Printed in U.S.A.

ABOUT THE AUTHOR

Victoria Chancellor married a visiting Texan in her home state of Kentucky thirty-five years ago, and has lived in the Lone Star State for thirty-two years, after a brief stay in Colorado. Her household includes her husband, four cats, a very spoiled Miniature Pinscher, an atrium full of tortoises, turtles and toads, and lots of visiting wild critters. Last year she was blessed with both a new son-in-law and a granddaughter. Her former careers include fine jewelry sales, military security and financial systems analysis. She would love to hear from you via her Web site, www.victoriachancellor.com, or P.O. Box 852125, Richardson, TX 75085-2125.

Books by Victoria Chancellor

HARLEQUIN AMERICAN ROMANCE

844—THE BACHELOR PROJECT
884—THE BEST BLIND DATE IN TEXAS
955—THE PRINCE'S COWBOY DOUBLE
959—THE PRINCE'S TEXAS BRIDE
992—THE C.E.O. & THE COOKIE QUEEN
1035—COMING HOME TO TEXAS
1098—DADDY LESSONS

Don't miss any of our special offers. Write to us at the following address for information on our newest releases.

Harlequin Reader Service
U.S.: 3010 Walden Ave., P.O. Box 1325, Buffalo, NY 14269
Canadian: P.O. Box 609, Fort Erie, Ont. L2A 5X3

To my son-in-law, Dale Renno,
for making my daughter happy and giving us Lilly

Acknowledgments:

Thanks to my neighbor and friend Pris Hayes,
vegetarian and community activist, and my cousin
(of some sort!) by marriage Cody Marshall, genuine
Texas cowboy. Any errors or exaggerations are mine.

Chapter One

Raven York turned off the engine of her aging green Volvo wagon, but Pickles wasn't quite ready to stop running yet. She coughed and sputtered a few times, then obediently fell silent. With a feeling of disbelief, Raven stepped out of her car into the vast Texas prairie. Her long skirt and hand-dyed scarf billowed in the warm breeze as she pocketed her keys and retrieved her tote bag from the passenger seat.

"I can't believe I'm supposed to be here," she whispered into the wind, but no one else was around to comment.

She'd never seen a more unwelcoming place in her life, and she sincerely doubted that a garden could have survived here for nearly a hundred years without careful tending.

The house wasn't the Ponderosa, but it wasn't Green Acres, either. It looked rawboned and bare, as if there had never been a woman around to soften its harsh edges or brighten up the drab beige of both painted wood and brick. Even the roof was taupe. Shadows from the front porch, supported by outdated aluminum scroll columns, nearly hid the brown front door and windows. Front steps ended in a sea of unmowed grass and dead tufts.

Surrounding the house, blue, red and yellow flowers

dotted the rolling hills, but at the moment, all she could think about were the countless cattle gathered beyond the fence. She'd seen their poor, sad, white faces as she drove toward the house. Doomed. They were Hereford steers and their days were numbered.

She watched the cattle graze and felt as if she should cry, but she couldn't, because she had to get to the bottom of this mix-up. Had she taken a wrong turn someplace? She'd followed the directions carefully. All the landmarks matched. The country roads had been clearly marked, and she'd made a right just past the big lopsided cottonwood tree that had been split by lightning.

Surely the Society for the Preservation of Heritage Gardens would not have sent her to a working cattle ranch.

Raven crushed the woven jute handle of her tote and took a deep breath. She vaguely heard a door closing, which meant people were around somewhere. Well, she'd just march right up to the door and get some answers. Maybe she was jumping to conclusions. Maybe things weren't what they seemed…

And then she spotted the tall, lean cowboy who stepped out of the shadows. With his crossed arms and angular, set features, he might as well have shouted, *Go away,* instead of silently leaning against one of those ugly aluminum columns and staring a hole through her.

Raven's stomach felt as if she were still on the bumpy narrow road that had brought her from the state highway to this ranch. She pressed her hand to her middle as she stared back at the cowboy. Why didn't he wave or come to greet her?

She forced herself to walk calmly toward the hostile-looking house. Surely there had been a mistake.

She smiled tightly. "Hello, I'm Raven York. I may have taken a wrong turn. I'm looking for the Rocking C."

"You've found it," he answered, pushing away from the aluminum column.

She looked back toward the pasture where the cattle grazed and felt her smile fade. "Really?"

"I'm Troy Crawford. Call me Troy," he drawled, unwinding his arms and taking a step toward her. Upon closer observation, he wasn't really threatening. His handsome face appeared intense, and he looked as if he were just a fraction as confused as she was.

Sometimes she got a feeling for things that others didn't. A couple of her friends who professed to be psychic claimed she had a "gift," but Raven went along with her pal, Della, who said that some people were just more observant than others.

"So you're the expert the association sent?" he asked.

"Well, yes, I do have experience—"

"I hate to tell you this," he said with a smile that didn't reach his eyes and wasn't reflected in his voice, "but you just don't look the part." He gazed pointedly at Pickles, then turned his disapproval on her, giving her a thorough inspection from the top of her curly black hair to the toes of her canvas sandals.

It stunned her how he could be so insulting with just a glare. "I was thinking the same thing about your ranch."

"What's that supposed to mean?" he asked with a frown.

She pulled herself a little straighter and tightened her hold on the jute handle. "Your ranch doesn't look like the kind of place where my services would be needed."

"For one thing, maybe the association didn't tell you but this isn't really *my* ranch. My brother runs it, but he's in the military. The Rocking C has been in my family for a little over a hundred years, though."

"Oh, I see." Not that she really did, of course. He was confusing and cryptic, and all she wanted to do was get to the bottom of this assignment.

"My brother Cal asked me to take care of the place while he's gone, and he asked the association to send someone to *help* me."

He said the word *help* as if he didn't believe he needed any. Or didn't believe the person his brother sent would be any use.

"I haven't been a rancher in fifteen years," he added. "I'm a marketing director for Devboran cattle. It's a new breed, a cross between beef Devons and African Borans, so you might not recognize it. Normally, I live in Fort Worth, but I'm on the road a lot."

Raven frowned. "I see, but why did you need me?"

"I already told you," he said, giving her another one of those not-quite-sincere smiles as he reached for her bag. "I'm not a rancher. I've taken a leave of absence from my job to help out my brother."

She held on for a moment too long, before realizing he was pretty intent on dragging her big tote into his house. She let go and he opened the door.

I'm not a rancher, either! she felt like shouting. Instead, she ignored the building's unwelcome vibes and followed him inside.

"You might not be a rancher, but you look like a cowboy."

He turned back with an amused look on his face. "Yeah? And how is a cowboy supposed to look?"

That smile could melt butter in January, she thought as she peered at him in the dim interior light. He was definitely handsome. At a little over six feet of lean muscle, long legs encased in the requisite jeans and scuffed boots on what must be size-twelve feet, he sure looked as if he could ride and rope and…whatever else cowboys did.

"I'm not sure, I suppose. I'm from New Hampshire."

His smile faded and he looked at her as if questioning her response. "Okay, then."

She wanted to say, *Okay, what?* but for the sake of getting off on the right foot simply followed him into the eat-in kitchen. The large square room seemed to be the hub of the house where the hallway came together with the living spaces.

The kitchen was just as dreary and outdated as the exterior of the house, with beige vinyl flooring, dull brown cabinets and faded floral wallpaper. The pseudocowboy staring out the back windows appeared far more interesting than the decor.

"Can I get you a glass of water or a soda?"

"No, I'm fine, thank you."

"I suppose the association mentioned that I have a guest bedroom for you here at the house. Is that okay?"

"Yes, they did say I'd have accommodations on the property." She'd envisioned a quaint guest cottage surrounded by roses and bluebonnets. They hadn't explained that she'd be sharing a very isolated house with a handsome cowboy. She wasn't certain how she felt about that setup in the light of day, much less in the dark of night.

"Is anyone else living here?" Wife and children, perhaps.

"No, it's just me. Neither Cal nor I are married."

"I see." So, they would be alone.

"My bedroom is down the hall," he said as if reading her thoughts. "You'll be at this end of the house with your own bathroom."

"All right." They wouldn't be sharing a bath, but she was near to the kitchen and living areas. Not as private as that nice guest cottage she'd envisioned.

"I grew up here in this house," he said, cutting into her wandering thoughts. "I left for college and haven't worked on a ranch since I was eighteen."

"Do you miss it?"

He paused a moment too long. "No."

"Oh. But—" She hurried to catch up as he turned down the hallway to the left. What did he study in college? Did he miss his job? How long was he taking off?

And why was she so interested in a brooding Texan who was so difficult to read?

"This is your room," he said, placing her tote bag on the double bed. The brown coverlet had probably been put there before Troy Crawford left for college. The off-white walls hadn't been painted recently, either, and the dresser and nightstand were of some type of dark wood. Nubby beige drapes hung from a sagging rod.

She looked back at Troy Crawford and found him watching her. "It's not a five-star hotel, but I imagine you've stayed in worse."

"Oh, I wasn't... Sorry. The room is a surprise. I wasn't sure what to expect. It's just that I've never stayed in a ranch house before."

"What?"

"Most of my work has been done east of the Mississippi."

"I wouldn't think there were many ranches that needed your help back there."

"Ranches? No, but there are lots of homesteads, some with three or four generations still living on the same land that was settled in the 1700s."

He frowned. "Why would you care about historic homesteads?"

She frowned right back, more confused than ever. "Because that's how I glean much of my knowledge."

"About their cattle?"

"No," she replied slowly. "About their heritage gardens."

"Gardens? What are you... Wait a minute." She watched an entire evolution of expression transform his face. "You aren't a ranch expert, are you?"

"Of course not! I'm a vegetarian. I'm against eating beef. Any kind of meat, for that matter."

Troy Crawford rubbed a hand across his face. "I knew there was something wrong."

"Just as I did when I arrived on a working cattle ranch!"

"Wait a minute. Why did you think you were here?"

"To document and restore a heritage garden."

"A what?"

"A garden used by settlers to provide herbs, fruit, vegetables and beauty."

"Dammit. I need a cattle expert."

"Well, the last place I want to be is on a cattle ranch. I'm looking for old roses and tomatoes, daisies and berry bushes. Ranching is against everything I believe."

"Then you are definitely in the wrong place."

"What did I just say?"

He turned away and looked up at the dingy popcorn ceiling. "Well, we'll go call the association and get this straightened out."

"Sure. There's probably a simple explanation."

"The cattle guy is probably in the next town, wondering why there's an old garden and no stock."

"Right. And the person who needed my help is probably

wondering why the man on their doorstep knows more about feed than seed."

"Okay then. Let's get this cleared up."

She followed him out of the gloomy guest bedroom, relieved she wouldn't be staying there for two weeks.

TROY SETTLED BACK IN THE desk chair and willed himself to be patient. "I know I'm not the person who requested the expert. I'm the brother. Cal Crawford is in the military, in Afghanistan. That's Calvin P. Crawford IV for the record. He contacted you via e-mail and requested a cattle specialist to come out to the Rocking C in Brody's Crossing, Texas." He'd told this story already, to the receptionist. Sweet girl, but she hadn't been helpful, either. "The expert showed up today, right on schedule, but she's a *gardener,* not a cattleman."

"Mr. Crawford, we don't send out gardening experts. Everyone who's a member of the Farmers' and Ranchers' Society deals with livestock and related issues."

"I know that, but I'm telling you, the person who is here knows nothing about cattle. Do you have a record of Raven York? She's from New Hampshire, for crying out loud!" Hardly cattle country.

"Let me check."

Troy wedged the phone between his shoulder and neck while he listened to bad elevator music. He hoped they remembered he was on hold. While he waited, he booted up the computer but then remembered that there was only one phone line in the house, and he was currently using it. He couldn't get on the Internet to check his e-mail via the antiquated modem and that increased his frustration level.

Dammit, he understood why Cal thought Troy needed

help. He hadn't lived on this ranch—on any ranch—for a long time. But any number of neighbors could have come to his aid, as they'd offered since he'd been back to the area. He'd seen them when he went into town, although he didn't have much time to socialize. He had three ranch hands who worked according to Cal's instructions, but they didn't have the training or experience to run a ranch on their own. They couldn't make decisions about breeding or culling the herd, or changing feed or buying hay if needed.

The elevator music stopped. "No, we don't have a record of Raven York as a member or a paid consultant. Are you sure that's her name?"

"I didn't ask for ID, but that's what she said."

"She's not from our association. Maybe she was sent by someone else."

"Any idea who would send a Yankee vegetarian animals rights lover to a Texas cattle ranch?"

"Er, well, no."

"Have you ever heard of the Society for the Preservation of Heritage Gardens?" Troy asked.

"No, I haven't."

Troy scrubbed his hand over his eyes. "Is there anyone else at the office we can check with?"

"Yes, but he's on the phone right now."

"There's just the two of you?"

"This isn't a big association. To be perfectly honest, we're a little old-fashioned."

Join the club, Troy felt like saying.

"We specialize in the general farm and ranch, whereas a lot of the groups are more specific to a breed or a type of operation. We support the family ranch and do our best to keep the traditions alive."

That sounded like something out of a brochure, but Troy didn't point that out, since he was in marketing himself. In his real job. When he wasn't getting a headache on his family ranch. Thankfully, his assistant back in Fort Worth was handling most of the day-to-day duties, and Troy could advise via phone or e-mail when necessary.

"I know. We raise Herefords, and our father was a member, and my brother since our dad passed away. But I'm more interested in the specific request my brother made. *He asked for a ranching expert.* He's paid dues for years and all he's gotten so far is a bimonthly magazine. We need help, and we need it now."

"I'm sorry, Mr. Crawford, but I don't see any request. I'll have to talk to Mr. Sam Goodman, the general manager, but he's still on the phone. I'll give him the information you told me and we'll see what we can find. He's been running this association since the 1970s, and he has a terrific memory."

For someone who'd been working at the same job for the past forty years and is probably past retirement age, Troy wanted to add. "Just get back to me as quickly as possible. Ms. York wants to find out where she's supposed to be, and I need to locate my ranching expert before the end of the day."

"We'll sure do our best."

Troy gave the man the numbers for his cell phone and the ranch phone, then hung up. He'd detected no sense of urgency, despite the fact it was Friday afternoon. He doubted Mr. Goodman or anyone else worked over the weekend.

"Any news?" his non-cattle-expert asked from the doorway of the office.

"No. I called the association in Bellville. That's a little town northwest of Houston. They've never heard of you and the person I talked to didn't have any record of Cal's request. Hopefully, the senior guy will know something, but he's busy."

"Is it a big association?"

"No." Of course not. A big association would charge a lot more money and would not have a list of retired volunteers who took on assignments for peanuts. A big association might have a list of top-notch consultants, but they would charge thousands of dollars for helpful advice. Troy really didn't think the person Cal had asked for could save the ranch, but dammit, it had been Cal's decision. Troy felt as if he owed it to his brother to try this approach…first.

"If I could use your phone, I'll call my contact at the Society for the Preservation of Heritage Gardens. It's a small group, too, but maybe we'll have more luck getting answers."

"Good idea." Troy handed her the ancient phone that had sat on the desk for at least thirty years, then got up from the chair and stepped aside. "Have a seat. I'm going to grab a soft drink. Would you like one?"

"No, thank you. I have some water."

She probably didn't drink soda anyway. She was around average height, a little on the slim side, but not that two-hour-on-the-StairMaster trim that he observed in some other women. In Fort Worth, he often saw artificially plump lips, small noses and hollow cheekbones. They didn't look all that real, especially when combined with large breasts on skinny women. Raven York seemed natural, as if she never thought about her looks, just her comfort.

But, heck, what did he know? And why was he spending any time thinking about it, since she'd probably get her answer and be gone by sundown.

RAVEN DIALED THE NUMBER OF the society that was working with the heritage homestead back home. They were a small group located in Florida, but had some excellent members who were willing to help with research and restoration. The project near her New Hampshire farm was especially important because there wasn't another authentic homestead like it open to the public in her area. Schoolchildren would really benefit from seeing a working homestead from their ancestors' era.

As soon as the phone-answering system kicked on, Raven started to worry. She dialed the director's extension, and listened to a slightly feeble voice on the recording.

"This is Mrs. Margaret Philpot. I will be out of the office on Friday afternoon and all weekend visiting my grandchildren. I should be back in the office late Monday or Tuesday. Please leave a message and I'll get back to you as soon as possible."

Oh, no! "Mrs. Philpot, this is Raven York. You sent me a letter and instructions about coming to Brody's Crossing, Texas, to the Rocking C ranch to document a historic homestead garden. I'm here, and the owner of the ranch knows nothing about a garden. As a matter of fact, he was expecting a cattle expert! Please, we're trying to figure out how this mix-up happened. Call us back as soon as possible."

She gave Mrs. Philpot the number of the ranch, which was neatly typed on the round insert in the middle of the old black phone. "Please, let her call back soon," Raven whispered, crossing her fingers.

"No luck, either?" Troy Crawford asked from the doorway.

"No, but I'm sure she'll check in for messages." At least, Raven hoped she did. Since Mrs. Philpot didn't leave a cell phone or other number, the odds weren't great.

"This is bizarre," he said.

Raven silently agreed.

AFTER WAITING FIFTEEN MINUTES and then placing another phone call to the Farmers' and Ranchers' Society, Troy felt his blood pressure rise a few notches. He put the phone down and turned to Raven. "Mr. Sam, as I've just learned they affectionately call the older gentleman who runs the place, will call me back as soon as they find out what happened to Cal's request."

"As my New England ancestors used to say, patience is a virtue."

"Right. So are a few other traits that I don't seem to be in possession of right now."

"Well then," she said, straightening up, "I'll just get a few things out of the car. I'm going to have a snack while we wait for the phone call."

"You're welcome to raid my fridge if you'd like."

"No offense, Mr. Crawford, but I doubt it's stocked with organic vegetarian food."

"Certainly nothing organic unless some mold has grown on the cheese."

She wrinkled her nose at his joke. Well, a halfhearted joke. The cheese probably *was* moldy.

"I'll just get my tofu and fresh fruit. I'm sure the ice I put in the cooler this morning is probably melting, and the tofu needs to be kept cold."

Tofu. He'd tried it once at a Japanese restaurant in Seattle. Bean curd had the consistency of slimy, firm pudding and tasted like…well, bean curd. "Help yourself to whatever you need." There was no reason to be inhospitable just because they were worlds apart in values and backgrounds. She seemed nice enough when she wasn't turning up her nose at cattle ranching.

"Thank you. And you're welcome to join me."

He tried to hide his own grimace. "Thanks, but I…er, gave up bean curd for Lent, years ago. I think I'll wait for that call."

"Of course." She turned in a swirl of skirts and scarves and long black hair. That woman sure was swirly. And when she got a little peeved, her cheeks flushed a nice shade of peach.

Not that he had any reason to catalog her looks. As soon as they got the mix-up fixed, she'd be gone. Or maybe before, if she decided to leave on her own. She had no reason to stay on the Rocking C, especially since she found cattle ranching so objectionable.

Troy rubbed his face for what seemed like the hundredth time today. He didn't need this. He needed help—whether arranged by Cal or himself—not criticism from a kind-of-cute vegetarian garden expert.

He unclenched his hands and stared at the phone, willing it to ring. He wanted to find out something before he e-mailed Cal in Afghanistan. If he was out on patrol or somewhere equally remote, he might not reply for days. Besides, it would only make him more concerned about the ranch if he knew the specialist he was depending on hadn't shown up.

Troy promised himself that he'd give Mr. Goodman half an hour, then he'd call back. If the senior person there couldn't help him, Troy would do some research on his own. Surely he could discover how this mess had happened.

After all, as his swirly-girly reluctant guest had suggested, there had to be some connection between the two completely different associations.

Chapter Two

"I can't believe neither one of us could get any answers," Raven said as she followed Troy from the home office into the kitchen an hour later.

He'd tried to call his association again, but with no luck other than the vague promise that they'd get back to him ASAP. The Internet hadn't yielded any results for them, either. There was no apparent connection between the two groups.

Raven leaned against the kitchen counter near the sink. "I can't believe Mrs. Philpot is the only person who can sort this out for me. This is just too bizarre."

He opened the refrigerator and took out a beer. "Tell me about it. Every day without the guy I was expecting is another day wasted." He held up the brown bottle for her to see. "Care to join me?"

"No. I'm too upset."

He took a long drink from the bottle. She watched his throat move as he swallowed the cold beer. Odd, but she'd never thought swallowing beer could be so…sensual. He lowered the bottle and asked, "What kind of arrangement do you have with the gardening folks?"

"I'm helping a local organization get a historic farm certified by the state. The property and house were donated to the township but had to be renovated. The construction is just about complete, and we're ready to plant the garden."

"But why are you here?"

"The township felt it was better to have someone experienced to plant the garden rather than getting the locals to do it. So I volunteered to come down here for at least two weeks and work in the garden while, in return, the Society for the Preservation of Heritage Gardens will restore a homestead garden near where I live in New Hampshire. It's rather like Habitat for Humanity, where people work in each other's homes and eventually get their own house."

"So you and your colleagues trade out time to help each other?"

"That's right. We're not paid. We're all volunteers."

"That must be tough—to take time away from your own jobs for two weeks."

"Some people do it on their vacations, but in my case, I have a good friend, Della, who is taking care of my farm. She has an apartment in the city, but we work together on a lot of fiber projects, so she's often at my place."

He finished the beer and tossed the bottle into the trash container in the corner of the kitchen, on top of newspapers, cans, coffee grounds and cardboard boxes. Why was she surprised that he didn't recycle or compost? She fought the urge to criticize his lifestyle.

"Surely the society will understand if there's been a mix-up. You can make new arrangements, can't you?"

She shook her head as she followed him across the kitchen. "You have to remember that our growing period up north is so much shorter than yours. We don't have time to reschedule. If I don't fulfill my obligation, the society could say that they won't send anyone to New Hampshire."

"Yeah, I can't wait for my expert to show up, either. My brother will be gone about six more months and I need to turn this place around. By the time he gets back, this ranch could be in big trouble if I'm on my own."

"Well, I'd hate to see your brother homeless, but I can't say that I'm sad a cattle ranch is going out of business."

He frowned at her as he opened the refrigerator. "You won't be so happy when you learn that I'd have to sell off all the stock, including the three little orphaned calves out in the barn." He removed several oversize plastic bottles fitted with big nipples.

She decided to ignore the concept of "selling off" the stock. "Oh, are you going to feed them? I love calves." She'd raised two calves from a neighboring dairy farmer a few years ago.

He rolled his eyes at her enthusiasm. "These are just orphaned beef cattle, and right now they need their supper."

"May I come with you? I have experience with calves."

He glanced at the clock over the old-fashioned stove. "It's already after five here, six o'clock in Florida, so I doubt we'll be getting any phone calls today." He started toward the door, then turned, nearly colliding with her. He pointed a finger. "Don't get any ideas about the calves."

She schooled her features and raised her eyebrows. "I have no idea what you mean."

"Yeah, you do, and I'm just warning you…"

"I'll consider myself warned, Mr. Crawford."

The sun was low and bright in the western sky as they stepped outside. Raven shielded her eyes as they strode toward the big whitewashed barn. She used the walk to calm herself down after Troy's scolding about the calves. He certainly had a way of getting under her skin.

She should probably leave to find a motel room before the sun set, but she wanted to look around just a little before she left the Crawford ranch for good. There might be interesting differences between New Hampshire and Texas farms. She tried to learn from each place she visited.

"What's that?" she asked as she hurried to keep up with Troy's longer stride. She'd hoped to find a garden, even one in terrible disrepair, behind the house, but there was none. Only a few wildflowers competed with the tufts of grass.

"The smokehouse," he told her as he continued across the yard, "but I don't think it's used anymore."

"Why is that?" Raven asked, even though she had little interest in the answer. She seriously doubted the Crawfords smoked vegetables.

"Cal lives here alone and I don't think he entertains a lot. He doesn't need to smoke that much meat. Back when my grandparents lived here, I think they sold what they smoked."

"Oh. Did they have a large family?"

"Just one."

"Your father?"

"Right."

Raven fell silent as they neared the barn. A small flock of white leghorn and Rhode Island Red chickens scattered around them, then immediately went back to chasing grasshoppers and scratching for seeds. The breeze brought the sweet scent of horses and their feed, of fresh hay and manure. The smells were familiar and reassuring, and for a moment she almost forgot she was on a cattle ranch.

"How about you?" Crawford asked, stopping at the barn. It was as if he'd suddenly remembered to be conversational. "Do you have a big family?"

"No," Raven said slowly. She didn't like to recall her childhood and there wasn't anything about her single mother that Raven cared to share with strangers. "I'm an only child. My mother lives in Manchester, New Hampshire, while I have a small farm in the country."

He opened the door and motioned for her to go inside. "Watch your step."

"Thanks," she said as her eyes adjusted to the low light inside.

"There are some horses here that Cal and the ranch hands use to work the cattle."

"Oh. I heard that some ranchers use all-terrain vehicles, or even airplanes, to handle—or perhaps I should say harass—their herds. I can't say I agree with those methods. Horses are much more ecofriendly."

He frowned and narrowed his eyes but didn't respond to her gibe. "The Rocking C isn't big enough for a plane, and as for ATVs, well, Cal is a real traditionalist."

There was a note of disapproval in Troy's voice when he spoke of his brother's ranching methods.

"I'll get those calves fed."

"Oh! Poor babies." Sad, orphaned little calves. They had no mother, and although they didn't know it, they didn't have any future, either. She had an urge to comfort them. She always felt more grounded when she was with animals, especially the ones who needed her. The ones starved of affection.

He gave her a look that told her he wasn't as sympathetic to the calves' plight. "Remember, they're beef on the hoof. When they're old enough, they'll join the herd. *I'll* see to them."

"You don't think I should care about your precious 'beef on the hoof,' as you so charmingly classify them, do you? Even if they are just babies."

"They're calves, not babies, and the answer is no."

"I'm only trying to be helpful."

"These are my brother's animals and my responsibility. You're only here until we get this mix-up straightened out, remember? You don't need to get attached."

"A little kindness can't hurt them."

No, but it could hurt you, Troy thought as he saw the yearning in Raven's expressive face. Did the woman not know how to hide her emotions? She was too softhearted by a mile, and despite her occasional scathing remarks about cattle ranching, apparently hadn't learned to put up barriers to keep from getting hurt by life's realities.

Out here, deadlines and budgets and physical limits didn't allow him or his ranch hands the kind gestures and gentle sentiments Raven liked to indulge. The bank loan had to be repaid from the sale of the cattle, and you sure as hell couldn't think about the cattle's *feelings* when you were out to get a good price per pound on the hoof. And what if the drought didn't break or a tornado hit the buildings or a hailstorm smashed through the ranch? The cattle could become infested with insects or disease might wipe out a herd. Too many bad things could happen in a heartbeat to speed the end of the Crawford family ranch that Cal spent his life trying to preserve.

Or maybe Raven lived in some sort of fairy-tale land in New Hampshire. Maybe she'd never faced the real world. Growing up on a cattle ranch had toughened him up fast, especially after his mother had left the intolerable dynamics of the Crawford family—not to mention the harsh realities of ranch life—for greener pastures.

"Look, I don't want to argue with you. I'm going to feed the calves. If you really want to help, you can give each of the five horses half a scoop of sweet feed and a scoop of oats."

"You keep them in the barn all the time?"

"No, they're in the stalls today so the *ranching expert* could see them." He shook his head. "Normally, if they aren't working, they'd be in the pasture."

"I'll be glad to feed them," she said. "Where do you keep their grain?"

He pointed out the tack room, the feed room and the tiny bedroom that at one time had been occupied by a wrangler. Now, its single bed, nightstand and straight-back chair was even more dusty and dingy than the furniture in the house, and all the workers lived elsewhere. Even the bunkhouse, which at one time housed a half-dozen cowboys, was falling in on itself.

Much like the economic structure of this ranch…

Raven went off to see to the horses. Within fifteen minutes Troy had the calves fed, although the ungrateful beasts had managed to get milk and slobber all over his clean shirt and jeans. He closed their stall door and found Raven looking him over, a slight smile on her face.

"Is there anything else I can help you with?" she asked. He seemed a little worse for wear. Maybe the calves knew he wasn't all that sympathetic to their plight and had made him pay. Or maybe she was projecting a little.

"Not in those clothes," he said, eyeing her up and down, making her very self-conscious.

"They're comfortable," Raven said in defense of her

chosen style. Full skirts, sweaters or tunics and sandals were so pleasant to wear, even if she did look as out of place as…well, a New Hampshire Yankee in the heart of cattle country.

"Did you bring something more practical for Texas?"

"Of course. But these are some of my favorite things. Most of the clothes I'm wearing were made by friends or myself. I knit and weave, but someone I know crocheted this scarf. Another sews vintage fabrics into new garments and crafted my skirt."

"Nice hobbies, I suppose, if you have the time."

She suddenly felt she needed to defend more than her clothing choices. His flippant words denigrated a whole group of people who believed in creating something beautiful and functional from natural fibers, not manufactured in cookie-cutter style from synthetic materials. But it wouldn't do any good to start a philosophical argument here in the barn, so she explained through clenched teeth, "It's not a hobby for most of us, it's a livelihood."

"So you're part of an artsy-craftsy bunch back in New Hampshire? I thought you lived on a farm."

"I run a *working* farm, where we use what we produce. You're making it sound as if we're frivolous."

"No, I'm not," he said with a smile.

"Yes, you are, and I don't appreciate your constant condemnation of my lifestyle."

He shook his head. "Lady, I don't know enough about your lifestyle to condemn it, even if that was my intention, which it's not. So don't get on your high horse about *my* attitude. It seems to me that you're just a little too defensive."

"Oh, so now my food, clothing *and* opinions are wrong!"

"I didn't say they were wrong. They're just not…normal for Texas."

"The entire world does not revolve around Texas!"

"I know that, but lots of folks down here don't feel that way, so you might want to rein in your Yankee sentiments and eccentricities."

"I am true to myself, Mr. Crawford, and that's not something that I can change."

"Well, good for you. I hope you aren't planning on a long stay or forming a lot of close relationships with Texans."

"I came here to do a job, not to make lots of friends." She paused, then lifted her chin. "Although, I must admit, I'm very good at making new friends. I have them all over."

He raised an eyebrow and asked, "Ever been to Texas before?"

"No, I haven't."

"Well, there you go." He took off across the yard.

"What do you mean by that?" She almost had to jog to keep up. White and red chickens scattered in their wake.

"Stick around. You'll see."

By the time she reached the back door of the house, he was holding it open for her.

"I think it's time for me to leave."

"Come on inside and we'll talk about it."

She stepped into the kitchen. "It's obvious we don't get along. Besides, it's going to be dark soon. I need to go into town and find a place to stay tonight."

"Um, it's not that easy."

"What do you mean?" Was he forbidding her from leaving? Was he *threatening* her? She knew he didn't like her, but really…

"There's not much in Brody's Crossing."

"You mean there are no hotels, no bed-and-breakfasts?"

"Not a one. There used to be a motel on the road toward Jacksboro, but it closed a long time ago. Of course, there are a few motels in Graham, if you want to drive over there. It's at least fifteen miles."

"Well, that's…unfortunate." She sighed and resisted the urge to slump. She'd come so far today she couldn't face driving to the next town. "Are you absolutely sure?"

"To the best of my knowledge, there's not even a room to rent in Brody's Crossing."

"Maybe there's something you don't know about."

He shrugged. "You can stay here," Troy said with a definite lack of enthusiasm.

"Really, I don't think you mean that, and besides, it's not a good idea."

"Why?"

"Because it's obvious you don't want me here. I'm not your ranching expert and I'm not a friend. You don't approve of anything I do, of who I am, so I think it would be best if we parted ways."

"I was just joking about the tofu."

"And my vegetarian lifestyle? And my clothes? And my friends with the frivolous little *hobbies?*"

"Okay, maybe I was a little hard on you, which I shouldn't be. I…I kind of know what it's like to be treated disrespectfully." He shrugged again. "Let's just say that I was joking."

"You were not, and I'd appreciate it if you didn't insult my intelligence as well as every other part of me."

"I didn't do it intentionally."

"If I may paraphrase an old western movie, this house ain't big enough for the both of us."

He laughed. "That's pretty good."

"Thank you. Now, I'd better collect my tote bag and cooler and get on the road. Again."

"That was a Willie Nelson song."

"What was?" she asked as she walked down the hall to the depressing guest bedroom.

"'On the Road Again.' Do you know it?"

"No, not really. We don't listen to much Willie Nelson on our artsy little vegetarian farms."

She grabbed the heavy tote bag from the brown bedspread, and when she turned, Troy Crawford was blocking the door, his forearms resting on the door lintel.

"I'm sorry I was rude to you. Sometimes I joke around when I'm really pis—um, I mean upset. I wasn't lashing out at you as much as at the situation."

"I'm just as upset about this mess, but I'm not attacking your choices."

He sighed and looked down at the floor. "Well, you did say you didn't mind if the ranch failed, but that's no excuse, I guess. I'm really sorry. Will you accept my apology?"

"Gladly. If you'll allow me to walk out that door."

"You're free to go, but I'm telling you, there's no place *to* go. Look, if it would make you feel better, you can have the house to yourself. I'll stay in the barn."

She sighed. "Thank you for the offer, but I don't want to put you out. There must be somewhere to stay. Perhaps I could use your phone to call?"

"You're free to use the phone as much as you want."

She carried her bag to the door and looked up into Troy Crawford's face. "Thank you."

He lowered his arms, stepped back and reached for the jute handle. "You're welcome."

Instead of arguing about who would carry the bag, she handed it over and followed him to the study.

"Just answer one question for me," he said, pausing at the door and turning back to look at her.

"Okay."

"Why don't you have a cell phone?"

She sighed. "I had one until two days ago."

"What happened?"

"The goat ate it."

"The goat?"

"Billy. He eats everything," she said with a sigh. "Once he ate my purse while I was talking to a friend, and I didn't even notice until the strap fell off my shoulder."

Troy laughed, but she didn't think it was funny that her cell phone was now in a compost heap in New Hampshire.

"I didn't have time to replace it before I left for Texas." *Much less the money, since it wasn't insured.* "Now, can I make those calls before it gets any later?"

Fifteen minutes and several phone calls later, Raven was finally convinced that there weren't any motels, hotels or bed-and-breakfasts in or around Brody's Crossing. She probably should have believed Troy Crawford, but it had seemed so unlikely that there was no place within a reasonable distance where she could rent a room. That was unheard of in New England, but she remembered all the wide-open spaces along the highways as she'd driven through Oklahoma and Texas, so she supposed it made sense in the West.

She sat alone in the Crawford home office and wondered what she was going to do now. Accept his hospitality, grudging though it might be, or...what? Money was somewhat tight. She could sleep in her car, but where, and for how long? Besides, the weather was so hot!

And really, where was the need, when Troy Crawford had offered her his guest room? He'd even volunteered to sleep in the barn, for goodness' sake! The hot, dusty barn. She'd taken a peek inside the small bedroom out there, and she wouldn't wish it on anyone. It was even more depressing than this bare-bones, no-style, outdated house.

"Did you find a place to stay?" he asked, startling her as he leaned against the door frame. The man was so silent. He didn't hum or whistle or stomp around.

"No, as I'm sure you knew. As you'd warned me."

"So are you going to stay here? I've got to tell you, it's a long drive to anywhere, especially at night."

She sighed. "I know it is. Besides, maybe Mrs. Philpot or Mr. Sam will call or e-mail with some answers."

"Perhaps, but I wouldn't bet on it until Monday."

"I know."

"Well, then, I'll get my things together. I'll go out to the barn to sleep, but I have some work to do first."

She might regret this in the morning, but she couldn't put him out of his own home. She faced the other wall and absently folded the length of her scarf. "No, you don't have to stay in the barn. I mean, this is your house. If you wanted to get in, you could. I'm sure there are keys. I feel safe with you in the daylight, so I'm certain I'll feel equally safe at night."

"You're sure?"

He said the words so softly that she had to look back at

him to see his expression. Unfortunately, he gave nothing away. Just that softer than expected question.

"Of course," she said briskly, letting the scarf slip through her fingers.

Chapter Three

Raven pushed away from the desk and stood up. "I'll be glad to help with dinner."

"Um, are you sure you can cook?"

"I cook for myself all the time!"

"I doubt I have any of the ingredients you're used to."

"I doubt that you do, either. Fortunately, I brought a supply of food until I can locate organic vegetables."

He shook his head. "Good luck with that. Most folks around here believe in 'better living through chemistry.'"

"I'm sure there are some people who grow their own produce without pesticides or chemical fertilizers."

"If you say so."

"I'll track them down."

He held up a hand. "I wish you more luck than you had finding a motel."

She took a deep breath, ready to argue some more, but all the steam when out of her. He was probably right about the vegetables. After all, he was from round here. She was the visitor, the outsider.

This was not a role she relished. She hadn't enjoyed being considered "different" when she was a child, and she didn't like it now. Back in New Hampshire, she fit right in. She had friends, business associates, acquaintances. She had like-minded e-contacts around the globe.

But in Texas, at least in this part of the state, she was definitely odd.

"If we can't prepare a meal together, may I at least use your kitchen? I promise to clean up after myself."

"Of course. I'd fix you a meal, but you probably wouldn't eat it."

She swallowed her affirmation. "I'm sure you're a fine cook."

"Beef, beef and more beef."

"Yuck, yuck and more yuck. Do you ever think about how cruelly the cattle are treated?"

"It barely crosses my mind. And really, that's a small part of their life. Most of the time, they get to graze in a pasture, hang out with their friends and eat all they want."

"Before they are suddenly taken away from everything they know and placed in an overcrowded, dirty stockyard, then prodded into a slaughterhouse!"

"Look, I think of animals as animals, and you obviously want to give them human emotions. We aren't going to agree on this. Can't we just move on?"

Raven wasn't so sure she could "move on" past his beef-obsessed views. However, she was a guest in his home and it was her duty to be more polite than she'd been.

"I'm sorry. You're right—let's just not discuss it."

"Right. Now, would you like to go first?"

"What?"

"In the kitchen. That way, it won't be…well, contaminated by my meal."

"I don't think your food is toxic. Well, not exactly. In the long term, perhaps."

"And there we were, getting along so well," he teased.

Raven sighed. "I'll get the rest of my food out of Pickles." She'd brought jars of homegrown food from New Hampshire—beans and potatoes, carrots, squash and vegetable soup—that she'd canned herself, plus bread and cheese she'd made. She'd been on one of these assignments before and knew she might not find any organic or wholesome food to eat.

"Pickles?"

"My car. Her name is Pickles."

He muttered something that she couldn't quite make out, and probably didn't want to.

"Won't be a minute," she said, scooting around the desk.

"I'll give you a hand."

"No, that won't be..." And then she thought twice. Those boxes and canvas satchels were pretty heavy, and Troy Crawford looked as if he could carry a lot on his big shoulders.

She reminded herself that she didn't really like overbearing men who could pick up whatever, whenever they wanted. As if they were superior because they were stronger than nice intellectual males. And she especially didn't like men who made teasing remarks about important issues!

All right, that was better. She was much more centered now. She and Troy had *nothing* in common, and even if they did, he wasn't an academic or an artist.

"Yes, thank you," she finally said. Being a gracious houseguest was much harder than she'd anticipated. She only hoped they could keep being civil to each other until the mix-up was resolved. Somewhere around here was a garden that needed her help, and she was going to find it before she bid a not-so-fond farewell to Texas—and Troy Crawford—forever.

RAVEN YORK WAS TRYING WAY too hard to be cooperative. Besides, she was too cheerful in the morning. She bustled around the kitchen before dawn making tea and toasting some dark, yeasty bread she'd brought from New Hampshire. As he'd filled bottles with milk for the calves, she'd asked twice how she could help him.

She wanted badly to feed those calves. He knew it, and he was standing firm.

"If you really want to do something, make a decent pot of coffee," he finally answered as he pulled a flannel shirt on over his T-shirt.

"I don't drink coffee."

"I do, but I'm not good at making it. So, like I said, if you want to be helpful, learn to make coffee."

"I can do other things, too."

Like feeding calves. "I've got it covered." Being personable this early was too tough to handle, especially without decent coffee. He'd never admit it to anyone in Brody's Crossing, but he missed his double-shot latte with the morning paper at the coffee shop near his condo in Fort Worth. He missed Starbucks in the airports when he traveled. Raven York probably thought he was a cowboy through and through, but in the past fifteen years or so, he'd become downright civilized.

"I'll be back in half an hour," he said, "then I'm grabbing some breakfast and coffee, and heading out for the morning."

"Are you going to town?"

"No, the ranch hands will be here by then and we're going to saddle up and check the fences. It doesn't take much for the cattle to wander off."

"Oh, that would be a huge shame," she said with such deadpan sarcasm that he had to smile, but then he remembered why he had to get blisters on his butt.

"Yeah, until they get onto the highway and walk in front of a school bus full of children."

"Oh."

"Right. So, I'm checking fence."

"I'll attempt the coffee."

"I'd appreciate it."

As soon as the door closed behind Troy, Raven tackled the old metal percolator. Despite what she'd implied, she knew how to make coffee, she just didn't drink it. As a matter of fact, she'd worked for a short time as a barista in a coffee shop in Manchester during college. Of course, the Crawford ranch didn't have anything similar to the commercial espresso machine she'd used there. Still, a little cleanliness went a long way, and this percolator was proof that only men had lived here for many years. Now if she could just find some white vinegar and baking soda.

When Troy returned thirty minutes later, Raven poured him a steaming mug of coffee that even she secretly admitted smelled pretty good. Perhaps she'd see about some organic coffee beans…

"Thanks. What's that smell?" He blew on the steaming mug, smiled, then added, "I mean, it smells great."

"Almond butter on whole wheat toast, and scrambled eggs with a little goat cheese."

She watched his smile fade. "Oh. Like I said, it smells… great."

"It tastes great, too. Come on, be adventurous."

"I've eaten goat cheese before. It's just not my favorite. Give me a good sharp cheddar every time."

"I brought this all the way from New Hampshire. I make it on my farm."

"Okay, but it's still from goats."

She rolled her eyes and didn't try to convince him that her goats produced the best milk, and consequently the best cheese, around.

He washed his hands at the sink while Raven watched his back. His wide shoulders and the muscles along his spine moved beneath the soft shirt, making her wonder what he'd look like without it. Which made her angry at herself for getting distracted by a tight body.

"You're being awfully nice, cooking breakfast for me," he commented, his back still to her as he dried his hands.

"I'm a nice person."

"Even to cattlemen?" he asked as he turned around.

"I'm trying to be, but I'm not going to give up on changing your mind—on changing everyone's mind—that eating meat is both bad for you and for the animals it destroys."

"That fact is debatable."

"Not by me."

He sat at the table and picked up his fork, looking at the scrambled eggs as if they might suddenly jump up and run off the plate.

"You might as well taste them. The eggs have already sacrificed themselves for your breakfast."

"Oh, for heaven's sake! These aren't fertilized eggs. We don't even have a rooster."

"It was a joke. Not a very good one, I suppose."

"Joking about food is obviously not your talent. You do, however, make a good cup of coffee."

"Why, thank you."

He took a small bite, chewed, swallowed. Raven watched his jaw and throat move, watched the way the eggs slipped past his well-sculpted lips. She'd never thought eating scrambled eggs could be sexy, but apparently Troy Crawford accomplished that task with little effort.

"Not bad. The goat cheese is a little strong."

"It has a different flavor to cow's-milk cheese."

"Hmm," he replied, taking a bite of toast. He chewed, swallowed again, then said, "This is pretty tasty."

"If you eat eggs, milk products, nuts and beans, you can get enough protein."

"You're beginning to sound like a vegetarian commercial."

"It's what I believe."

"And I believe that ranching is an important industry in this state. In this country, for that matter."

"There are other, better uses for land. Some studies show that production of cattle consumes more resources than it generates."

"You can always find a study to support any theory."

"Doesn't it bother you at all?"

"No."

"But what about those calves? They're just babies—"

"I knew it! You're trying to save them."

She took in a deep breath and brought her chin up. "I'll save any animal that I can."

He walked over to the old percolator, refilled his coffee and raised his mug to her. "I'll consider myself warned." With that, he started to walk out of the kitchen.

"What are you doing now?"

"I'm going to finish my toast in peace, then e-mail my brother in Afghanistan that instead of the cattle expert he wanted, we're housing an animal-rights activist who intends to save his cattle from their cruel fate."

"I'm not an animal-rights activist! I'm a farmer who happens to love animals for something other than food."

"Right. That will make Cal feel so much better."

She didn't want to irritate Troy's brother while he was away serving in the military, even if he was a cattle rancher in civilian life. "Perhaps you shouldn't make your brother feel as if his ranch is being taken over by PETA."

"I'll keep that in mind. And believe me, you're not taking over."

He was right, Raven admitted to herself as he strode into the office and shut the door. She was simply a guest until she found out where she was supposed to be or until Troy Crawford got tired of her opinions and tossed her out. Either way, she'd better come up with a plan.

AFTER USING TROY'S PHONE to call home and check on her animals, Raven took a shower, dressed in a calico skirt and peasant blouse, laced up her canvas sandals and drove into town. Pickles puttered along the two-lane road with predictable coughing on some of the turns. After driving just long enough to wonder if she was lost, Raven came across the town-limits sign, and then in another minute or so, Brody's Crossing itself. She slowed down to the thirty-mile-an-hour speed limit as she passed a few run-down businesses and small homes, then a neat brick police station. She stopped on the corner at a flashing red light, right next to a bank that looked as if it could have been robbed by Bonnie and

Clyde. On the other corners were a drugstore, a café and the town offices.

She drove around the two blocks that made up the downtown, seeing some thriving businesses, such as the beauty shop and café, and some that had obviously been vacant for a long time, like a dress shop and a furniture store. And, near the train tracks, a boarded-up hotel that at one time had probably been very nice.

She drove past some tidy frame houses with gardens out front and picket fences defining the sides and backyards. Then the houses became fewer and the yards bigger, until she was once again in the country. Only a few mobile homes dotted the landscape now, and as Raven pulled off the road to turn around, she had to admit that finding a place to stay in Brody's Crossing wasn't going to be easy. *If* she was staying in town, which she wouldn't know until she talked to the heritage garden society.

The guest room at the Crawford ranch wasn't luxurious, but it was available. And free. And there was one perk that couldn't be duplicated even if she found a room for rent— Troy Crawford's very distracting body.

TROY STILL DIDN'T HAVE A reply from Cal, so he shut down the computer and leaned back in the desk chair. His brother must be out on patrol or whatever they did during the day now. He tried not to think about how risky life could be in Afghanistan or he'd fret all the time about Cal, who really hadn't expected to be called up or to be put in danger.

And Troy also had to worry about Raven, at least for a few more days. He didn't believe she'd do anything to sabotage the herd, but he knew she wanted to "save" them. Couldn't she understand that those Herefords were bred to be beef cattle and nothing else? That they were well treated, fed, wormed, and kept safe inside those fences that needed constant maintenance?

No, apparently she couldn't. And he didn't know how to get her off her soapbox about animal rights. All he wanted to do was look after this hopelessly antiquated ranch for his brother. Cal needed to have a place to come home to, not an eviction notice from the bank.

And Troy needed to know that he'd been the one to salvage the family ranch. Him. Not his father or his brother, but him. And if that was self-serving or arrogant or whatever, he'd just live with it. The old tried-and-true ranching practices were out of date. Maybe the association sending the wrong person was a sign that the time to act was now.

He pushed up from the chair. He'd been out riding fence in the one-hundred-degree heat. He stank and his butt hurt and he'd give one of his aching body parts for a thick, juicy steak and a baked potato. Which brought his thoughts back to his reluctant lodger. Where was she?

He looked in the guest room, kitchen and living room before searching outside. She was probably in the barn, knitting sweaters for the "poor little babies." If she got attached to those calves, he was going to...well, he didn't know what he'd do, but he sure as heck wasn't going to hold her and let her cry all over him when he'd warned her specifically not to get involved. Vulnerable baby animals could break your heart if you let them. She needed to toughen up, but he doubted she ever would.

On a hunch, before trekking to the barn, he checked the front of the house where she'd parked her Yankeemobile. Sure enough, it wasn't there. However, her canvas tote bag and clothes were still in the bedroom, so she hadn't left.

Good. She was just out running errands or something. Lecturing someone else on the evils of eating meat, no doubt. Winning friends and influencing people. Yep, that was Raven York.

While she was gone and the place was quiet, he took a much-needed shower and shaved, which he did every day whether he was going someplace or not. He had nothing against the scruffy look, although he couldn't stand the feel of stubble. He hoped Raven wouldn't think he'd cleaned up just for her. Giving her the wrong impression wouldn't be good for either of them, especially since she was only here for a few days.

He heard her close the back door just as he was checking his e-mail again. Still no reply from Cal. Maybe by tonight, which would be morning over there. Again he shut down the computer and went looking for Raven. He found her in the kitchen, rearranging things in the refrigerator.

"I wondered if you'd like to go into town to get a bite to eat in a little while," he asked. "I was kind of hard on you at breakfast, and well, you might find something you'd enjoy on the menu at the local café."

"Why?"

"I thought it would be nice to get away from the ranch for a while. You know, have dinner. Nothing more. No ulterior motive except to say I'm sorry for being rude. I'm not a morning person by nature and getting up before dawn is a stretch for me. Since I moved back to the ranch, I never had to get up early *and* be polite at the same time."

"I'm sorry my presence is so disruptive. I tried to find someplace else to stay, but you were right. There's nowhere. Believe me, I looked."

"You want to leave that bad?"

"Well, I know I'm not what you were expecting. I'm sure if the heritage garden people phoned you'd let me know, no matter where I was staying. And I get on your nerves, as you've pointed out. I'm not shy about my beliefs."

"Yeah, I got that." He ran a hand around his neck. "Look, the truth is, since you arrived, things have been a lot more…interesting. Sometimes it gets kind of boring out here. You might irritate me occasionally, but you're not boring."

"Well, thank you very much, I think."

He breathed a sigh of relief. "You're welcome. So can we go to dinner? About five o'clock? The café closes early."

"TROY CRAWFORD! HOW THE heck are you, son?" the booming cowboy asked as he squeezed Troy's shoulder. They were sitting in one of the booths that lined each long wall of the café. Front windows faced Commerce Street, and the order desk and window to the kitchen made up the fourth side at the very back. Raven had hoped that the café wouldn't be busy this time of day, but a surprising number of people were here for dinner.

"I'm fine, Bud. How are you?"

"Couldn't be better, unless beef prices go up and gas prices go down." The older man chuckled and looked at Raven. "I see you've got someone new in town."

"Raven York, this is Bud Hammer. He's a rancher."

Raven extended her hand. "Hello, Mr. Hammer."

"Just visiting our city boy, hmm?" he said with a knowing grin.

"Just a professional visit to the Crawford *ranch*," she replied.

"Professional? What's the problem, Troy?"

"Nothing serious. Ms. York is a consultant. She's giving me some new ideas...for crops and feed, mostly."

That was sort of true, she realized. They'd talked about what plants and products she thought everyone should eat.

"Oh." Bud winked at Troy. "Whatever you say."

"This is not a social visit." Raven fixed her eye on Mr. Hammer. She absolutely would not have anyone thinking she'd come to Texas for a nonprofessional reason, no matter how good-looking Troy Crawford was.

"Quit teasing the young folks," another older man said, clapping Bud on the back. "Who are you to question someone who's an expert?"

"That's right," his companion, also about retirement age, added. "Troy ought to know what he's talking about, since he works in the cattle industry."

"Thanks, Mr. Maxwell. Hello, Rodney."

"Call me Burl, Troy."

"I still remember you as Mr. Maxwell, my math teacher. It's hard to call you by your first name."

"We're all in the same boat now, aren't we?"

"I'm going to get some dinner," Bud said, "since y'all are having such a happy reunion."

"Have a nice one," Troy said, although Raven could tell he wasn't sorry to see the man go.

"I'm Rodney Bell. My spread is a little west of the Crawford ranch. We've been neighbors for years."

"And as Troy mentioned, I'm Burl Maxwell. I teach math at the high school and sponsor the 4-H Club."

"Hello, I'm Raven York," she introduced herself to the two men. "I'm pleased to meet you."

The men smiled. They seemed genuinely nice. "How are you enjoying your visit to Brody's Crossing?" Rodney asked.

"It's very…different than New Hampshire," she answered with a smile. "Troy has been a gracious host."

"Cal asked me to get a consultant out to the ranch," Troy explained. "Raven got sent here by mistake, but we're making the best of it until we get the mix-up fixed. She's trying to reform my wicked cattleman ways, and I'm trying to keep her from running off with all the calves."

Both men laughed, but Raven felt surprise that Troy had divulged so much to them. And a little annoyed that he'd made her seem so very different. So odd.

"I specialize in heritage gardens," she explained.

"That's great," Burl Maxwell said. "Too many of the old plants are being lost to modern hybrids and genetically engineered varieties. There's a real art in traditional methods of cross-pollination and grafting."

"Exactly! I'm so glad to find someone who shares my enthusiasm."

She could practically feel Troy roll his eyes, but even Rodney Bell didn't seem put off by her passion for plants.

"I remember back in the day," he said, "the Crawford place had quite a vegetable garden, plus there were some climbing roses. You know, those little pink ones that have quite a smell?"

"Probably a floribunda," Raven commented.

"Troy's mother tried her best to keep it going, but you know, after…"

"Then she was gone, and I imagine the garden was completely lost," Troy said, his tone flat.

Raven turned to look at him. His jaw seemed tight and his shoulders tense. What was the story with his mother?

"Well, we'd best get some dinner, too," Burl said, breaking the uncomfortable silence.

"You're welcome to join us," Troy said.

"Thanks, but we'll let you young people talk."

"I'd value your opinion on some of my ideas for the ranch," he said. "If not now, then how about coffee in a day or two?"

"It'd have to be after school," Burl said.

"Throw in some pie and you have a deal," Rodney added.

"Tuesday, then? Around four o'clock?"

"Sounds good to me."

"See you then."

The two men smiled and went back to another booth. They didn't join Bud Hammer, Raven noticed.

"Nice guys," she commented.

"Good neighbors, too. Maybe I'll get some ideas from them, just in case the ranching expert doesn't show."

"That might be a better option anyway, since they know the area."

"You'd think that, but it's not what Cal wanted."

"Do you have to do it Cal's way?"

"Cal's way or the highway," Troy scoffed. "I shouldn't be mean-spirited about this, but Cal is hell-bent on keeping our father's traditions, down to the last, ill-conceived detail. The ranch is struggling, but all he cares about is having things the same as they've always been."

"It must be frustrating for you."

"Believe me, it's beyond frustrating. Do I upset my brother while he's dodging land mines and snipers in Afghanistan, or do I contribute to the failure of our family ranch?"

"You have to do what you feel is right."

"Easy to say, not so easy to do."

"If it were easy, he would have done it already."

"Nothing is simple when it comes to my family." He opened the menu, cutting off the conversation. "I think you'll find something here to eat. They have some pretty good vegetables and a decent salad."

"I'm sure I'll be fine." But as she looked at her menu, she wondered if Troy would find some solution he could swallow when it came to the ranch.

Chapter Four

As Monday's bright, hot sun sank lower in the cloudless sky, Troy had to admit that Raven was a hard worker. He'd assumed she might want to sit around the house and knit all day, but instead, she'd tackled housekeeping chores when she wasn't helping him in the barn or exploring the property.

When he'd asked her why she was cleaning his house when she was a guest, she explained that she felt she should earn her keep since she wasn't the consultant he'd been expecting. He'd insisted that wasn't necessary, but she'd wanted to help, and he hated housework so much that he let her.

He'd done his best to keep her away from the calves, but he was pretty sure she snuck out there whenever he or the ranch hands weren't around. He'd spent much of the weekend on his horse, checking the two wells farthest from the barn. Windmills pumped water up into rock troughs, but sometimes the old plumbing failed, or the cogs broke. That's the kind of thing that happened with ancient equipment—not that Cal would think of replacing the fifty-year-old machinery.

Wincing from his time in the saddle, he dismounted outside the barn. Before he could catalog all his aches and pains, Raven stuck her head out of the barn door. "Oh, you're back. I was just wondering if I should fix dinner."

"What were you planning on making?" he asked carefully. He'd learned to be...reserved around her food after she'd explained what she'd brought with her from New Hampshire. He'd seen a couple of the meals and several snacks she'd made for herself. They seemed more like rabbit than people food, and much of it smelled like old goat.

"A vegetable pasta that's really quite tasty. I found some organic tomatoes in town today and I thought I'd serve those with a balsamic vinaigrette."

"No goat cheese?"

"Not unless you want some."

"I'd rather not." He'd eaten goat cheese in several high-end restaurants, but he hadn't liked it any better there than in Raven York's scrambled eggs.

"That's okay. So, I'll head on in and get supper started."

"Sure," he answered, pushing his reservations about dinner aside as he led his gelding into the barn. At the end of the long day, the horse seemed to have more energy than he did. Or maybe it was worry that was bringing him down.

He still hadn't heard from Cal, and even though it was Monday, the ranch association hadn't contacted him on his cell phone. Of course, someone could have left a message at the house. He'd check that as soon as he got inside. He wanted all these unresolved issues put to rest as soon as possible. Unfortunately, he still didn't know how to save the ranch.

He stretched his back, shrugged his shoulders high and rotated his neck to get the kinks out. His damp shirt pulled and clung to him as he rolled each shoulder, relieving the tension and the hours in the saddle.

Raven stood just inside the door, watching him.

"Is something wrong?" he asked.

"No! I just…I'm going in right now."

She turned and hurried off, her plain skirt swirling around her legs and her long curly hair blowing in the breeze. She gathered the mass into her hand, twisted it and draped it over her shoulder.

She sure had a lot of hair. He wondered if it was soft to the touch—as soft as the breeze that blew over the top of the hill even on the hottest day. Or was it wiry and strong, much as he supposed Raven was?

And why was he standing here wondering about her hair anyway? He should be taking the tack off his horse, turning him out, getting a shower and thinking about dinner. But no, he was calf-eyed over his temporary houseguest.

A few minutes later, he entered the kitchen and placed his boots next to the back door, just as his brother and father had done every day of their lives on this ranch. The kitchen was filled with good smells for once—pasta sauce and tomatoes and balsamic vinegar. He could go for that type of dinner, even if it wasn't served with a twelve-ounce T-bone.

He wondered if Raven could whip up a cheesecake for dessert. Probably not. She didn't seem to like sweets or normal milk products, so sugar and cream cheese probably hadn't found their way into his kitchen.

"I'm going to hit the shower after I check the answering machine to see if we got any messages. Thanks for making dinner. When will it be ready?"

"About fifteen to twenty minutes," she answered, looking over her shoulder from the stove. She gave him a quick glance.

He probably looked a sight in his scruffy jeans and long-sleeve shirt, his feet in white tube socks that had seen better days.

"What would you like to drink?"

"I'll grab a beer after my shower."

Raven watched Troy walk out of the kitchen, his damp shirt clinging to his wide back, the pockets of his soft, worn jeans moving against his tight butt. She'd never seen a man who looked so good after working hard all day.

And now he was going into the bathroom to get naked.

Just then, her pot of water boiled over, sending sizzles and sputters and steam all over the stove. She snapped out of her fantasy about her host to move the pot to an empty burner and grab a towel. How ridiculous to be influenced by an attractive body, she chastised herself as she mopped up the mess. A strong back didn't indicate a strong character, just as a pretty face didn't mean a person had a beautiful soul.

Of course, she had to admit that Troy had at least offered—no, insisted—that she stay at the ranch when he could have kicked her out after realizing she wasn't a ranching expert. And she was irritating. She knew that, but she couldn't prevent herself from speaking her mind any more than she could stop her gaze from wandering..He was nice much of the time, although he made some snippy comments. But so did she. Maybe they were about even.

Daydreaming didn't get dinner on the table, so she pulled herself together and got busy fixing the rest of the meal. By the time Troy came back into the kitchen, she'd set the table and placed the steaming dish of whole wheat penne pasta in the middle, between the vinyl place mats she'd found.

"That actually looks pretty good," he commented after taking a long-neck beer from the refrigerator and twisting off the cap.

"Thank you."

"I don't suppose those white chunks are chicken."

"No, of course not! They're tofu."

"Tofu," he said with a moan. "I was hoping to get away from that stuff."

"You need protein after working all day."

Troy sighed. "At least it's not goat cheese."

LATER THAT EVENING, WITH all the animals fed and bedded down, Raven settled on the couch with her knitting while Troy took the big, well-worn recliner. He seemed absorbed in reading the *Cattleman Magazine,* so she concentrated on not feeling homesick as she threaded beautiful indigo-and-walnut-dyed wool through her fingers.

Unfortunately, with every click of her knitting needles, she remembered making this yarn. She and her friends had sorted the fibers after her sheep had been sheared last spring. Her buddy, Wallace, who lived in nearby Manchester with his boyfriend, clipped the animals by hand every year. Wallace might not be interested in women, but he was nice to look at, since he took quite a bit of pride in his muscular body. She and Della would stand back and watch as he removed his shirt, pulled the sheep between his knees and went to work with the shears. She suspected he shaved or waxed his chest, but she'd never asked, and he'd never volunteered such information.

She was pretty sure Troy Crawford didn't wax anything, or shave except for his face. She paused in her knitting to look at him. Now he had a little line between his brows, and she wondered if he had a headache, was worried or just not feeling well. She knew he had a lot on his mind, with his brother gone and the family ranch in trouble. He'd also mentioned that he was still adjusting to riding long hours and working outside all day.

He looked up and asked, "What's wrong?"

"Nothing. I was just thinking."

"About what? You looked as if you were really concentrating."

Her mind raced. She sure wasn't going to admit she'd been thinking about *him*. That would send the wrong message, and she didn't want him to ask her to leave because she couldn't make him believe that she was just worried about his general health and well-being.

So she reverted to her original musings. "I was remembering my animals and friends back home. I miss them."

"I suppose you have lots of animals."

"I do. I have sheep and rabbits that I raise for wool, and milk goats and the billy goat I already mentioned. Plus there are my pets, Mr. Giggles, who's a Dutch rabbit, and Ms. Pris, my cat. They all keep me busy."

"I'll bet they do. You probably give each one of them individual care, don't you?"

"Of course. They may be animals, but they depend on me for everything. I make sure they're more than just fed and housed. It's important to me that they're happy."

"How do you know they're happy? You could be assuming that's their reaction because that's what you want it to be."

"I suppose we all do a bit of projecting, but I do know that they seek me out. My sheep come to the fence when I talk to them. They have few diseases or injuries because they live in peace. The shearing is the only stressful event in their lives, but they recover from it very quickly and afterward, they enjoy being scratched. I tell them that they don't look odd, and that I'll use their wool to make beautiful yarn to keep people warm."

Troy rolled his eyes, which didn't surprise her. "We don't have the same kinds of farms down here that you do in New Hampshire."

"You could. There's no reason a farm can't be a happy and harmonious place."

He flipped open his magazine again, breaking eye contact. "If nothing else works, maybe I'll try your approach. I'll ask the cattle to put on a lot of weight so people can be well fed."

"That's just mean."

"Sorry," he said, although he didn't look a bit sorry as he smiled slightly before hiding behind the magazine. "I guess I'm not so good at making jokes."

No, he wasn't, and she was now even more homesick for her pets and her friends. If Billy hadn't eaten her cell phone, she'd be calling Della and getting some much-needed sympathy.

THE NEXT MORNING, TROY fixed scrambled eggs for the two of them after doing the morning chores in the barn. For himself, he fried a half-dozen strips of good, thick bacon. He also made toast from some bread Raven had bought in town.

"Good morning," he said when she entered the kitchen from the bathroom. He'd heard the shower running as he'd poured himself a cup of coffee from the pot she'd made. She might be a raging vegetarian, but she could sure brew coffee.

"Good morning." She hid a yawn behind her hand. This morning she wore a more normal outfit—a solid light blue

T-shirt tucked into a pair of jeans, which surprised him. A lot. And they looked good on her, too.

"Nice jeans."

"I thought they might be more suitable for Texas."

"They might be. Turn around."

"What?" She sounded a bit outraged.

Troy laughed. "I need to see the pockets."

She glared at him then reluctantly twisted around. "What about them?"

"Just as I suspected, they aren't Wranglers or Levi's. That's what cowgirls in Texas wear." He had to admit, though, that the little swiggly embroidery across the back pockets did a nice job of bringing attention to a perfectly rounded butt. He'd had no idea she had such curves hidden under those swirly, loose skirts and tops.

"I'm not a cowgirl and never will be."

"Okay, but I'm just saying…"

"I'm only dressing to be comfortable and appropriate."

"If that's the only reason you're getting dressed, then feel free to go around au naturel if you'd rather."

"Very funny, Mr. Crawford. Now, what's that you're fixing for breakfast?"

"I made some scrambled eggs and toast for you. The eggs are from our ranch chickens, with no pesticides or antibiotics. I'm having bacon, of course, since I'm an unrepentant carnivore."

"Bacon! It's full of chemicals and salt, not to mention the hormones they use on the pigs. Bacon will kill you faster than almost any other meat."

"Yeah, but I'll die happy, with a full stomach."

"You're impossible."

"I know, but I'm healthy as a horse, so just stop attempting to reform me. It's not going to happen."

"I have to try."

"Watch out, Raven," he said with a grin. "I'll start to think that you care."

"I care…about the animals."

"Ouch! Well, if that's all, then sit down and I'll serve your eggs."

She took a seat, managing to appear girly even though she wore work clothes. She'd look better still if she added a nice belt with a shiny buckle. And some good-looking boots with a riding heel wouldn't hurt, either.

Not that he was really fantasizing about her.

"Thank you for breakfast," she said after taking a few bites. "This is quite good."

"You're welcome. So, what do you have planned today?"

"I'm going to phone the heritage garden society since they haven't called me. Or you. And then, unless I have some answers, I'm going into town. I need some things."

"Like decent cowboy boots?"

"Of course not! I don't wear leather shoes."

"Ah, that explains those canvas things you've got on."

"Yes, but I have hopes that I can find some vinyl boots."

"They don't fit as well, look as good or hold up as long," he said, taking his last bite of breakfast.

"Perhaps not, but tell that to the cow."

He rolled his eyes. "Okay, let's not argue. If you want to use the office phone, go ahead." He stacked his plates and took a last sip of coffee.

"I'll clean up the dishes since you cooked."

"Thanks."

"Naturally, you'll have to dispose of that obnoxious

grease from the bacon first." Just when he was starting to think nice thoughts about her, she had to ruin it with another comment about one of the many things he held dear.

"Naturally," he said, shaking his head as he headed for the skillet.

"And have you thought about starting a compost heap? I could help you while I'm still at the ranch."

This time he slapped his forehead as he headed for the back door. Compost heap. Like he had time for that.

RAVEN WAS SO FRUSTRATED AFTER failing to get any answers from the heritage garden society that driving into town felt like the only possible action. Mrs. Philpot wasn't going to be back to work that week because she'd caught a rather nasty stomach virus during her visit to her grandchildren. The mystery of the garden/ranch mix-up would continue, unless Troy had better luck.

Raven parked Pickles in front of Casale's grocery store on Main Street, near the end of the downtown area. She'd bought tomatoes here yesterday. Today she needed more supplies, especially since it seemed she would be at the Crawford ranch for at least another few days.

After getting a cart, she roamed the aisles, looking first at fruit and vegetables, none of which was marked organic. As she'd done yesterday, she found the produce manager and asked what was locally grown.

"Same as yesterday. We have tomatoes from Ida Bell's garden, and this morning she brought in some greens."

Raven didn't remember him mentioning the name of the person who'd supplied the homegrown vegetables. "Is she related to Rodney Bell?"

"He's the husband. They have a small ranch just north of here. You know them?"

"I met Rodney at the café the other evening."

"Nice man. Nice couple."

"Are you sure she doesn't use pesticides?"

"I can't say for one hundred percent certain, but that's my understanding. If you want to confirm it, you should go see her."

"I may do that. I'm a big advocate of all-natural food and organic produce."

"I got that impression, miss."

"My name is Raven York. I'm from New Hampshire."

"I figured you weren't from around here."

"I'm just in town temporarily…on a special project."

"On a cattle ranch."

"That's right."

The produce manager shook his head. "Surprising."

"Tell me about it," Raven said, picking out some leaf lettuce, kale greens and tomatoes.

After looking for more of the wholesome items on her list, she found the assistant grocery manager and made some suggestions on what they should carry in the future. She finished her shopping, finding some organic whole wheat flour, but no all-natural brown rice or fettuccine. She may have to make her own out at the ranch, not that she expected Troy to own a pasta press. She could wing it, though. Like her New England ancestors, she knew how to work with almost nothing to fix good food. And besides, growing up she'd had to "make do" too many times to count. Her single mother hadn't been able to provide everything they'd needed, and it was either improvise or depend on the kindness of others.

And charity was highly overrated, at least if you were on the receiving end.

She decided to ask Troy how to find the Bell ranch. He was supposed to meet Rodney Bell and Burl Maxwell later today to talk about improvements to the ranch.

As she drove down Main Street, she decided to stop for lunch. Apart from the café they'd eaten at the other night, there was only the Burger Barn. She doubted they served anything she would eat, so the café was the only option. She parked a few doors down from the intersection and walked in the pleasant heat of a May morning. Several people were out, and most of them were heading to lunch, it seemed.

She arrived just after a group of three older ladies were given the last booth. Even the five stools at the counter were taken.

"I'll seat you as soon as we get a table or stool free," the waitress told her, hurrying by with two large glasses of iced tea.

"I can wait." She really had nothing else to do. Troy was out riding fence again today, so she couldn't argue with him. Or ogle him. Not that she should spend time on either activity.

She stood there for a minute or two, glancing around, taking in the people and the place. In her hometown, this diner might have been more wood than metal, more stone than concrete. On the menu, there would have been some items made with maple syrup, not chicken-fried steak or catfish. But when you were a stranger anywhere, people looked at you pretty much the same way.

"Excuse me, young lady, but would you like to join us?"

Raven looked around to see who was being addressed and realized the woman was talking to her. She hadn't been called "young lady" in a long time, if ever. "Thank you, but I wouldn't want to interrupt lunch with your friends."

"Oh, we have lunch almost every day. We'd love to have someone new to talk to, wouldn't we, Bobbi Jean?"

"Absolutely. Please, come join us. Tell us all about you."

Raven smiled, walked around the half wall dividing the entry from the first booth, and slipped in beside a blonde who was probably around sixty. The two women on the other side of the booth had salt-and-pepper hair and sparkling eyes, and looked as if they enjoyed life. "I'm Raven York."

"I'm Bobbi Jean Maxwell," one of the ladies opposite said.

"I'm Ida Bell."

"You supply the grocery with fresh vegetables, don't you?"

"Yes, I do. I love to garden and always grow more than we can use."

"I'm so glad, because I've been buying your tomatoes, lettuce and kale. I'm a vegetarian and I prefer organic produce. I wanted to meet you."

"I don't like chemicals, either."

The blond woman next to Raven said, "I'm Clarissa Bryant. I run Clarissa's House of Style, just down Main Street."

"It's nice to meet all of you, and thank you for asking me to join you. As you might have guessed, I'm new in town. Just here on an assignment, actually."

"You're the young woman who's staying with Troy Crawford out on the ranch, aren't you?" Clarissa asked with a smile.

"Well…I'm staying at the ranch, but I came down here to restore a heritage garden."

"On a cattle ranch?"

Raven thought she'd scream! If one more person implied that she had no business being on a cattle ranch, she just might. "There was a mix-up. I'm waiting to find out where I'm really supposed to be."

"Well, there are worse places to be in a mix-up than on the Crawford ranch. That Troy has grown up to be a fine-looking man," Bobbi Jean observed.

"That's for sure," Ida confirmed.

Thankfully, the waitress came by then to take their orders. Raven hid behind a menu, studying the limited choices while the other ladies ordered. "I'll have a BLT, hold the bacon, and could I have fruit instead of chips?"

"One dollar extra."

"Fine." That was a small price to pay to avoid trans fat. She'd become an expert on trade-offs in life. You could have a happy home life or a real learning experience, for example.

"If you're here to fix a garden, you must know a lot about plants," Bobbi Jean said, bringing Raven back to the present. She nodded.

"Okay, how much do you know about those so-called all-natural cures? Do they really work?" Bobbi Jean continued. And during the next thirty minutes, she and the older ladies had a very informative and interesting lunch.

When she drove out of town with her groceries and the phone numbers of her new friends, the last thing she expected to find was another misfit looking for a place to stay.

Chapter Five

Troy arrived back at the ranch around three o'clock, when the sun was really hot and he was really tired. He'd been in the saddle most of the day, but his body was getting used to the abuse. Any day now, he might become bowlegged, but at least his butt didn't hurt as much.

He looked forward to a hot shower and a cold beer, maybe not in that order, before he made his way into town to meet up with Rodney and Burl at the café. He hoped they had some good ideas for how he could improve the ranch.

After taking the tack off his horse, rubbing him down and turning him loose in the pasture to roll, he went into the house. Beer first, he decided, grabbing a cold one from the refrigerator on his way to the bathroom.

Some odd noises seemed to be coming from down the hall. Maybe Raven had the radio or TV on. Or maybe she talked to herself. He hadn't noticed that before, but then, he hadn't been around her all the time.

Her bathroom door was closed and there was lots of bumping and splashing coming from inside. Some moaning. Whimpering. This might be interesting if she was in the tub, alone and naked. But no, he shouldn't go there.

Then she said, very loudly, "No," and without thinking anymore about her saying "yes, yes," he opened the door.

Suds clung to the beige tiles surrounding the matching tub, and in the middle of the floor knelt a very wet Raven— unfortunately, not naked—and a very large, wet dog.

A dog? "What the hell is going on?"

She looked up, soap bubbles clinging to her nose and damp strands of hair surrounding her face, her expression one of startled guilt. Or, at least that's what he read there. The black-and-tan dog merely looked smug.

"What is a dog doing in the bathroom?"

"Well, I was using my bathtub to bathe my new friend."

"You can't have a dog. You're only here temporarily."

"What does that have to do with rescuing a dog?"

"Dogs chase cattle."

"Oh, don't be silly. This dog isn't going to chase your cattle, your chickens, or anything. He's very well behaved."

"Oh, I can see that. I suppose you flung the soap on the ceiling yourself."

She looked up, and appeared a little more guilty. "He was excited."

I'd be excited, too, if I were in the tub and Raven was soaping me down. The thought popped into his head before he could stop it. The canine commands "down, boy" and "no" seemed appropriate right now.

"He's been a very good dog on the drive to the ranch."

"He probably recognized a pigeon when he saw one."

"If you're referring to my compassionate, caring nature, I'll take that as a compliment."

"Look, there are loose dogs all over the place in the country. He probably belongs to someone."

"Would that be the someone who put a note on his collar

that read, 'Please give my dog, Riley, a good home. We can't keep him no more.' In childish handwriting?"

Troy ran a hand across his face, smelling defeat laced with a hint of damp dog. Still, he had to try. "He's probably infested with fleas, ticks and who knows what else."

"That's why I'm bathing him," she said with exaggerated patience.

"You, queen of the all-natural lifestyle, are using pesticides on a dog?" he scoffed.

She used her forearm to wipe sliding suds from her cheek. "I'm using natural organic shampoo and parasite controls."

"Which they just happened to have at the grocery or the feed store? In this town?"

"No, which I keep in the car, just in case I come upon an abandoned or injured animal."

Troy shook his head. "Of course you do. You would."

"You don't need to sound so offended by the fact I'm prepared."

"Honey, you'd put the Boy Scouts to shame. Who else travels with tofu, chickpeas and organic dog shampoo?"

She looked at him for a moment, as if she was trying to decide what he meant, then went back to shampooing the dog. "I'll just take that as another compliment."

"Take it any way you want, but you're not keeping that dog in this house. And please hurry up and rinse him off. I need to take a shower and be at the café at four o'clock." He turned and left the bathroom, shutting the door so the darn mutt wouldn't track water and soap and wet, angry fleas all over the house.

Not that it would have hurt this tired old home much. And not that she'd really listen to him, anyway. How had his life—his boring, frustrating life on the family ranch—gotten so far out of control in just four days?

TROY RETURNED FROM TOWN AS RAVEN WAS eating supper, her new friend curled up on a thick towel near the table.

"Are you ignoring my order that the dog has to go?"

"Of course. You told me that in a moment of distress. You didn't really expect me to turn away a homeless animal."

"Did he destroy anything while I was gone?"

"No, he did not! He's very well behaved, but a little shy."

"Shy? He's probably sneaky." Troy pulled out a chair and sat down. "What's your plan for the mutt?"

"His name is Riley," Raven reminded him as they sat across from each other at the kitchen table. "I think he's a border collie and retriever mix."

"Great. After he runs the cattle and chickens to death, he can bring them back to us. That will be so useful."

"You don't have to be sarcastic," she said, spreading a bite of hummus on the last of the wheat crackers she'd brought from New Hampshire. "See how nicely he's behaving?"

"He looks smug to me. I think he's just biding his time, waiting for the right moment to pee on the carpet or kill his first calf."

"Don't even say such a thing! From now on, Riley is a vegetarian."

"Dogs can't be vegetarians. They need meat. It's *natural* for them to eat meat."

"I don't eat meat, so Riley doesn't, either. I'm getting him a soy-based dog food tomorrow."

"At the grocery or the feed store?"

"If I have to, I'll have them order it for me."

"What are you feeding him until then?"

"He can eat people food for now."

"And what if you hear from Mrs. Philpot and you're off to someplace else? Who's going to pick up your soy-chow then?"

"Oh. Well, I'll see how long it will take for the order to come in. Mrs. Philpot isn't supposed to be back this week anyway." Raven took another bite, then asked, "Did you hear anything today from your association?"

"Only that they're waiting to hear from *your* association. The mix-up has them confused and intrigued. They claim to have no record of my brother's e-mail, yet he told me someone had confirmed his request, back before you showed up. Mrs. Philpot is the key, and unfortunately, she's busy worshipping at the porcelain altar."

"Crude, but accurate, I'm afraid." She finished her cracker and asked, "Did your friends come up with any good ideas for the ranch?"

"They promised they'd think about it, look up some numbers, get back to me. They didn't have anything concrete, and nothing I haven't thought about myself. I don't need suggestions—I need solutions!"

"But you have to start somewhere, right?"

"I have to start, period. This ranch is getting further and further into the red. If I don't come up with something, the bank will, and that's not fair to Cal." He paused, then added, "Hell, it's not fair to the memory of my grandparents or great-grandparents. They worked hard to keep this land, and now…well, it's in pretty bad shape."

"I'm sorry. Personally, I think organic is the way to go. It's a growing market."

"I don't think there are enough consumers to make it

worthwhile. It might work in smaller states, but this is Texas, the land of huge ranches and stiff competition."

"People want to know that they're getting something wholesome—even if they eat meat."

"Yeah, even them," he replied, obviously dispirited. "I guess I keep hoping for a lightbulb to go on over my head, for the answer to pop right up and be so obvious that I can't miss it."

"Inspiration is only part of the solution."

"Honestly, even if I'd gotten the expert my brother wanted, I doubt he would have found a way out of this right away. I'd still be in the same boat—looking to solve a problem that's been coming on for years."

"Your father must have been pretty stubborn."

"There's a picture of him in the dictionary, under 'bull-headed,'" Troy said, rearranging the salt and pepper shakers on the table. "And Cal is a chip off the old block."

"Not you, though."

"I've been told I take after my mother."

"Oh? What was she like?"

"Pretty. She had a lot of energy, a lot of dreams. I don't think she ever felt as if she fit in on the ranch, although she spent a lot of time with my grandmother. That was my father's mother. Granny C was something else. A tough woman. She had a hard life out here, living in the old ranch house."

He'd told Raven so much that was personal she didn't know what to say. However, one thing stood out; there was an old ranch house. Or at least there had been, not so very many years ago.

"Troy, do you know where the old place was? I was thinking that perhaps there is a garden out here somewhere."

"I don't think so. This house is the only one I've known.

They built it before I was born, in the late sixties or early seventies."

"You don't know where your grandparents lived?"

"I'm sorry. I don't remember."

"That's okay. I just wondered…"

"You're welcome to look around for a garden, but I imagine anything that existed is long gone. I showed you the smokehouse. There were more buildings, but I'm not sure where."

He paused and shook his head. "Ranch life is all about staying afloat, planning for the future but living in the present. I don't think the Crawfords spent a lot of time contemplating the past." He sighed. "This can be a hard life. It's not for everyone. Sometimes, there's only escape, one way or another."

"I'm sorry. You're talking about your mother, aren't you?" She didn't know if he meant his mother had run away from the hardship of ranch life, or if she had died.

"I don't want to talk about her," he said with some underlying anger, pushing out of his chair and away from the table. "So, where's the mutt going to sleep?"

"With me, of course. I don't want him to feel anxious in this new environment. He needs to feel at home."

"Raven, this is not his home." He opened the refrigerator and grabbed a bottle of beer. "Come to think of it, it's not my home, and it's not yours, either. This ranch hasn't been a home in a long, long time."

He walked out of the kitchen, leaving Raven alone in the silence, staring at the gathering darkness that had descended on the living room and hall. In just a moment, she heard the door to the office click shut.

At least now she understood why the house had seemed

so unwelcoming when she'd first arrived. And why all the rooms seemed so neglected, so bare. So sad.

Just like Troy Crawford.

LATER THAT NIGHT, AS RAVEN took her bath and prepared for bed, Troy walked through the kitchen to make sure the back door was locked. The steady *thump-thump-thump* of Riley's tail on the vinyl-tile floor brought his attention to the dog, who had appropriated the throw rug for a bed.

"So, you're all settled in," he said to the mutt who, he estimated, could be anywhere from a year to two years old.

Riley whined.

"What did she feed you?" Troy asked, knowing it wasn't beef, chicken or anything else a dog craved.

If she was adopting the darn dog, she had to give it something more substantial than granola and a few bites of goat's-milk cheese.

"I happen to have just what you need," he said, opening the refrigerator. He took out a package of reduced-fat all-beef bologna—his favorite brand—and peeled off a few slices. "Here you go, boy. Don't tell Raven or we'll both be in trouble."

Riley gulped down the meat and wagged his tail, his brown eyes wide and shining in the light from the open refrigerator. Troy found some chicken-fried steak he'd brought home from the café the other day and gave that to the dog, too.

"That's it," he said, then realized he was doing the same thing he'd accused Raven of last night—talking to animals as if they were people.

"That's what?" she asked from the doorway. A towel was wrapped around her head, leaving her neck bare. She had a really nice neck.

He grabbed the two percent milk carton. "That's the last drink of milk I'm having before going to bed."

She peered around the open door. "You're drinking from the carton? Eeew."

"Hey, you don't drink cow's milk anyway."

"I don't drink *your* homogenized, chemical-packed milk, but still, that's so unsanitary."

"This from a woman who picks up strange dogs," he said to Riley, who looked expectantly at the refrigerator. "You're such a girly-girl."

Raven folded her arms under her breasts, all bundled up in a cotton robe. "Come on, Riley. We're going to bed now."

Troy shut the refrigerator and watched her walk barefoot down the hall. He suddenly felt envious of the mutt. Going to bed with Raven, indeed.

THE NEXT DAY RAVEN DROVE into town with a cleaned-up Riley. "We're just going to double-check that no one is looking for you," she explained to the dog. "And we'll get you some good dog food. You're going to appreciate being a vegetarian, but maybe not at first. It's an adjustment. I have faith in you, though."

Riley seemed to smile as she looked back at him. He'd settled into the backseat as if he'd always been driving with her. She rather hoped he didn't have anyone looking for him, especially since he hadn't been taken care of very well. She'd cut a rope and the note from his thin, flea-infested neck yesterday. A child or simpleminded adult might have owned him, but they obviously couldn't look after him. She could, or she'd find him a good home.

Instead of leaving him in the hot car with the windows rolled down, where he might escape while she was in the grocery, she drove to the feed store. She'd used an old belt Troy had given her as a collar, and a corded belt of her own for a leash.

The feed store had a sitting area where several older men were drinking coffee and talking. They stopped when she came into the store. The smells of animal feed and seed had soaked into the wood for years, she could tell. The familiarity made her smile.

"Hello. Does anyone recognize this dog? I found him on the road to the Crawford ranch yesterday."

"I don't know it," one of the men said. "'Course, lots of dogs look alike."

"He had a note, but not the name or address of his owners."

"Sorry, miss."

"That's okay. I wanted to see about getting him some soy-based dog food." Riley seemed to perk up and smile for the men.

"We have some of that."

"Really!"

"Bella Fraser feeds it to her basset hound."

"Yeah, and boy, does it give him gas."

"Hush up, Claude," one of the men said. "There's a lady present."

"Sorry, miss." The man named Claude got up from his chair and ambled toward the door. "I've got to get back to the gas station, anyway." He turned and looked at Raven. "You mind my words, though. That food don't agree with every dog. Get him a bag of regular old Purina."

"I'll keep that in mind," she promised. "I need a collar and leash, too, please. Do you have something besides leather?"

Soon she was opening the trunk for the feed store proprietor to load a twenty-five-pound sack into the car. Riley jumped into the backseat, and Raven slid behind the wheel. "We're off," she told the dog as they drove around the block, down Main Street, and turned back to go to the ranch. Riley hung his head out of the partially open window, and even Raven felt pretty good about the day.

Her feelings changed abruptly when she had to pull over to make room for a huge tractor trailer passing on the opposite side of the narrow two-lane road. As she slowed, she saw that the trailer part was actually a cattle truck. The animals were packed into the double-deck rig, their red- and black- and white-colored bodies flashing by. Every now and then she glimpsed their big brown eyes, fearful and confused, as the truck carried them away from the ranch where they'd spent all their lives. They'd grazed contentedly in the pasture, slept under the stars and been as happy as a cow could be. And now they were being taken to their death.

Raven didn't realize she was crying until Riley licked her cheek. She'd stopped at the side of the road. The tractor trailer was long gone, but the image of the cattle lingered.

"I'll be okay, Riley," she told the dog, wiping her eyes with her fingers. "The truck made me sad. I can't help it."

She pulled back onto the road and drove the rest of the way to the ranch in silence.

TROY HEARD FROM CAL—FINALLY. His brother wasn't happy. He wasn't all that understanding about the mix-up. And he absolutely didn't want to hear that Troy felt the ranch needed a major change *now*. By the time Raven and the dog arrived home, Troy didn't feel like talking.

One look at her sad face, though, and he just had to ask, "What's wrong?"

"I… Nothing."

"Come on. I know something's happened. Your eyes are puffy and your nose is red."

"Maybe I have hay fever."

"Maybe you should tell me."

"You won't want to hear it."

"Tell me anyway."

She sank onto a kitchen chair. Riley put his head on her knee. "I saw a tractor trailer full of cattle, and I knew where they were going. I feel…very sad."

Troy didn't need this. "Look, that's what cattle do."

"No, that's what's done *to* them."

"You never give up, do you?" He didn't want to argue. He didn't want to hear another vegetarian lecture. He just wanted to save this ranch.

"You asked, but you don't want to hear it."

He rubbed the back of his neck. "Today, I'm just a glutton for punishment."

"Besides me, who is punishing you?"

"My brother. I got an e-mail from him. He's been out on patrol for three days. Believe me, the last thing he wanted to read was my message saying the ranch is in even worse shape than he thought it was."

"Why doesn't he know what a mess it's in?"

"Because he simply won't let himself believe that the family ranch might cease to exist. He thinks that if our father made it work, he should also. He doesn't realize times have changed in the cattle industry."

"Has he ever done anything else?"

"No. Other than joining the reserves, this ranch has been his life."

Raven sighed. "It's not enough to have a piece of land

become your reason for being, and besides, he's trying to make a profit on something that is inherently sad."

"If we can't make payments to the bank to cover the loan for the operating costs, we could be in foreclosure before he returns from Afghanistan. *That* would be sad."

"It would be terrible for him," she agreed.

"Yes, but he insists he wants to keep things the same. Well, the same just doesn't work!"

"Perhaps it would be best to sell."

"To whom? For how much? You might have noticed that if there's one thing we have in this part of Texas, it's land. And our family's land is only good for ranching. You can't farm it because the soil is rocky and there's not enough water, and no one wants to build anything way out here because it's too far to commute."

"Sometimes things just don't work out," Raven said.

"That's no attitude. There *is* a way to make this work. That's why I need advice. I know you want the ranch to fail, but this is Crawford land. It's a matter of pride for Cal and it's a matter of responsibility for me."

"I'm sorry, but I don't think you want to listen to what I have to say."

"Not if you don't want to understand ranching, which apparently you don't."

"I don't want to understand your kind of ranching! I'm sorry it's your family business, and I'm sorry Cal is halfway around the world, but to me, it's about the animals, not the acreage."

"And to Cal, it's all about cutting costs and hoping for a break. A break in the drought. A break in the price of beef. It's like trying to make a living gambling in Vegas. There's no art to that, no challenge or skill."

She sat there quietly, petting the dog, and then asked, "Have you always been this competitive with your brother?"

"I'm not being competitive! I'm trying to be practical. Someone has to be."

"I think *you* want to save this ranch."

"No, I want this ranch *saved*. Cal's not getting it done. That means it's up to me."

Raven shook her head, then rose from the chair. "If you insist on raising cattle, I think you should go organic. Use more humane methods to get them to market. Maybe downsize."

"We're not making enough as it is. We can't afford to downsize."

"All right, but you did ask for suggestions."

"I asked for *help*. And as far as I'm concerned, I'm still waiting for help—from Rodney Bell and Mr. Maxwell."

She looked as if he'd kicked her dog. He rubbed the back of his neck, then said, "Okay, maybe I shouldn't have said that, but—"

"Don't apologize to me, and don't half apologize and then try to justify yourself. You've made yourself perfectly clear. If I had anyplace else to go, I'd leave here immediately. As it is, until I hear from Mrs. Philpot, I'll just try to keep out of your way. If that's okay with you, obviously."

"You're not in my way."

"Well, that's not how it sounds to me." She turned so fast that her black curls streamed around her head. She and the dog disappeared down the hall. He was left with the empty place where she'd just stood.

He hadn't meant to hurt her feelings. He hadn't meant to drive her away, especially since her arrival was the most interesting thing to happen since he'd returned.

Chapter Six

Raven brewed coffee the next morning while Troy was in the barn doing his initial chores before coming back in for breakfast. She didn't really want to make coffee for him, but considered it part of her "rent" for staying at the ranch.

As soon as she found where she was really supposed to be, she'd be out of here as fast as Pickles could take her. Then he could go back to his own stinky coffee.

When he came through the back door, she temporarily forgot her anger. His light brown hair was tousled, his T-shirt white against tan skin, and his jeans fit like they'd been made just for him. He carried with him the scents of the barn and outdoors, and for a moment, her heart skipped a beat and she just gazed at him.

"Good morning," he said cautiously.

"Good morning," she replied, then jerked her attention back to a few drips of spilled coffee and away from the distraction that was, and probably always would be, Troy Crawford.

He brushed past her, and she shut her eyes and tried not to smell all those enticing scents. Up close, she sensed that he'd just rolled out of bed, all warm and manly. He still smelled of the soap and shampoo from his shower last night.

"I really am sorry I made that remark," he said softly, so near she could almost feel the tickle of his breath. "Please don't be mad at me."

"I...I'm sorry I walked out of the room. I did get angry." She shook her head. "I'm working on being more serene, but it doesn't always come easily."

"You do a real good job of that." She wasn't sure, but she thought he touched a strand of her hair. "Yeah, I'd say you were usually real serene."

She opened her eyes and saw him place both palms on the kitchen counter in front of him. His hands were big and brown, and there were a few new scratches and nicks.

"I do admire your devotion to your brother and the family ranch. I know it didn't seem as if I did yesterday."

"I'm not all that noble, Raven. You were right that we were and still are competitive. Our father...well, I'm not sure he encouraged us to be. Maybe he was oblivious to it when we were growing up. Cal and Dad were always so close. Too close for me to have any room to breathe."

She looked into his eyes and put one hand over his. "Oh, Troy—"

"Don't start getting all mushy on me. I was a big boy, a teenager, so it wasn't like they were kicking a puppy. And to be honest, I wasn't the easiest kid to live with."

"Still, you were a child when you lost your mother."

"I was a teenage boy. I sure didn't think of myself as a child, especially when it came to girls."

"We're talking about your relationship to your father and brother, not your...romantic pursuits."

"Yeah, but my romantic pursuits are more interesting

than talking about hairy-legged guys and all that old family stuff," he teased.

She looked at him, sensing his sudden shift in mood, and knew her eyes were big and round. "I don't want to talk about your romances."

"That's okay. If you get curious, just let me know."

"I won't get curious."

"Right."

She spun away from the counter. Her canvas sneakers squeaked as she hurried to where Riley sat beside his food dish. "I'm going for a walk. Have a nice breakfast."

"Are you sure? I'll scramble a couple of eggs for you."

"No, that's okay. I'll have a granola bar on the way."

"I'll see you later, then."

"Yes," she said with forced cheerfulness. "Later." When she had herself firmly under control again. "Come on, Riley. Let's go." She grabbed his new collar and leash and headed for the door.

She thought she heard Troy's chuckle as it closed behind her.

Riley seemed happy to be outside, and Raven let him run. He sniffed around the chicken coop and barn, and when he started to go under the fence into the pasture where the horses grazed, she called him back.

He obeyed her pretty well. She wouldn't put his leash on unless she had to. They skirted the barn and followed the fence. She hadn't walked this way before. She hadn't felt the need to explore, or even to get away from Troy. Today, she did. She walked well past the barn, across some rocky terrain where a few scrubby mesquites were trying to grow and continued up a hill.

Treetops were visible over the rise, and she walked in

that direction, with Riley bounding ahead. He would probably be covered with burrs and have a few insect bites by the time they returned, but it would be worth it. He was having a good time. And as she walked in the morning sun, Raven decided she was feeling much better, too.

Since she hadn't gotten any exercise this past week, her legs felt a little stretched by the time she climbed the slope. She stopped to look around, calling Riley back to her. He paused, then resumed his sniffing, down the other side of the hill toward the trees.

"Riley, get back here," she said, hurrying after him when he went out of sight behind some bushes.

Here, partially covered with native grasses and weeds, lay the remains of an old building. "Riley, no! Be careful." There could be nails sticking out of the boards, or snakes hiding beneath. She loved all creatures, but snakes…she'd rather not cross them if she could avoid the situation.

Especially Texas rattlesnakes. The very thought gave her the creepy crawlies.

Breathing a bit hard, she grabbed Riley and put his collar and leash on. "It's for your own safety," she explained, but he wasn't buying it.

The gray weathered planks lay in a haphazard pattern, as if they had fallen at different times, for different reasons. Raven bent down and looked at the planed lumber, noticing the square nail heads right away. This was old. These nails had been produced well before the end of the nineteenth century. Her pulse picked up a bit. Perhaps this was the original homestead, or one of the barns. She poked around some more, Riley tugging at the leash. "Not now, boy. I'm afraid you'll get hurt."

She found a stick and used it to turn over boards and

push aside grass. To one side of the structure, half buried in dirt, was an old iron handle for a bucket. She poked around some more, finding broken glass, and then, toward the end of the collapsed building, a crumpled window frame and a smashed white plate.

"Ah-ha," she announced to Riley. "This was a house. I'm sure it was the Crawfords'."

Riley only wanted to keep exploring. Raven skirted the fallen lumber and continued around to what she assumed was the back. Another smaller structure had collapsed perhaps thirty feet away. The ground sloped down to a natural streambed. Cottonwood trees and more shrubs defined the area. "Come on, Riley."

The streambed was damp, but there was no running water. Still, it meant that there had been water at one time, even if only when there was a good rain. The land was low enough that the trees and bushes could access the water table beneath the ground.

That meant something could have survived out here, alone, untended, all these years. Her heart rate kicked up another notch. Could there be the remains of a garden? A garden planted by Troy's great- or even great-great-grandparents?

"I DON'T KNOW ANYTHING ABOUT the garden," Troy answered as Raven cornered him in the kitchen. He'd spent the afternoon cleaning out one of the wells, and, as usual, he was dirty, hot and tired. Still, he felt he had to take time to answer her questions. Excitement burned in her dark eyes. Even the dog seemed pleased, but agitated.

The light in Raven's face dimmed a little, then he added, "But I could try to find out."

"Really? Thank you, Troy." She reached up and kissed

his cheek. He barely had time to put one hand on her waist, then she pulled back. "I suppose I shouldn't have done that."

"No, it's okay. You're just happy." And he felt suddenly confused.

"Oh, I am. The garden is overgrown and half hidden by fallen lumber, but there are plants there from the nineteenth century. I just know it!"

"Well, that's good, right?"

"It's great! If there is no heritage garden where I'm supposed to be, if Mrs. Philpot sent me on a wild-goose chase to Texas and this really is a monumental mess, then at least I may be able to salvage the trip."

"I don't know how much I'll be able to tell you about the garden. There are some old trunks and boxes in the attic. There may be something there—plans for planting, receipts for seeds."

"Most of the time, settlers brought seeds from their previous home, or they exchanged them with other travelers."

"Yeah, I guess there wasn't a grocery or general store here for them to shop at back when the homestead was first built."

"I'm sure conditions were very harsh. At least back East we weren't separated by so many miles of prairie. We had more neighbors. We had more…settled areas."

"You mean civilization," he suggested.

"Well, yes. It was more difficult here because there were no existing schools and churches, the basis of western society."

"I know the history, Raven."

"Oh. I'm sorry. I didn't mean that I was the expert. I get carried away when I talk about the past. About how our ancestors survived and flourished."

"There was a lot more surviving than flourishing in Texas, I'll tell you that."

She smiled, and he felt a little lighter. A little less tired. "I'll check out the attic tomorrow, if that's okay. I need to get cleaned up to meet the guys at the café. They have some ideas for the Rocking C." Finally, perhaps he'd get a game plan going.

She turned away, reached up to get a glass from the cabinet and filled it with water. "That's great news. I hope they can help you."

"Me, too." Somehow, though, he got the impression she was disappointed. That he might save the ranch, or that the other ranchers were helping him? He didn't know Raven well enough to tell what she was thinking.

With a final look at her as she bent over, pulling burrs from the curly coat of her dog, he headed for the shower.

TROY DIDN'T LIKE HER SUGGESTION to turn the Rocking C into an organic farm, and he didn't want her to go with him to the café. His intense desire to save the ranch probably blinded him to other options. Blinded him to anything she suggested. She wondered if he'd decided on any new options for the ranch, but his concentration on the hockey game precluded conversation.

She looked up from her knitting. He sat in the big chair, his feet on a well-used ottoman. The television was switched to a sports channel. Apparently Troy was a hockey fan. He was watching the playoffs, which seemed odd. Shouldn't hockey be over by now, when the temperature was in the nineties? But no, back in New Hampshire, the nights were still a little nippy, the days pleasant. The trees were budding and the grass was green. It was one of the most beautiful times of the year, and she was missing it.

She started to feel a little lonely, without Ms. Pris, who liked to curl up beside her as she knitted, and Mr. Giggles, who hopped around the floor in search of who-knows-what hidden treat. She didn't need television when she could watch a curious entertaining bunny with a twitchy nose.

"What are you smiling at?" Troy asked her, turning down the volume.

"I didn't realize I was smiling."

"You were. Kind of wistful. Were you thinking of home?"

"Yes, mostly about my animals. I miss them."

"Now you have a dog. Does that help?"

"Yes, it does," she said, looking down at Riley, who was asleep beside the ottoman. If anyone were to look into the living room right now, they'd think Riley was Troy's dog. "I think he's tired from all the walking and exploring we did today."

"You know, before you mentioned the old homestead, I hadn't thought of it in years. I mean, I knew it had existed, but I didn't think of that old pile of lumber as the place where my great-grandfather was born."

"Our past is like that sometimes. It creeps up on us. It makes us think of where we came from, where we're going. What's important to us."

"This ranch was obviously important to my ancestors."

"Maybe," she said, breaking eye contact. She picked up her knitting, then looked back at him and added, "But maybe family meant even more than land and cattle. Perhaps who we love plays a greater role than where we are or what we do for a living."

Troy didn't answer right away. He looked at her for a

moment, his lips tight and his eyes narrowed. "If that's the case," he said finally, "my brother is in even bigger trouble than I thought." Then, focusing his attention on the television, he turned up the sound on the hockey game.

SHE WAS GETTING TO HIM. GETTING under his skin. Making him a little crazy, as if he didn't have enough on his mind. Troy slammed the door on the truck and gripped the wheel. He needed to *do* something. All this uncertainty, all this waiting, felt a hell of a lot like failure.

He jammed the key into the ignition and turned over the engine. Failure was not an option. In his real life, he was a success. If his father and brother had listened to him years ago, this ranch wouldn't be in such a mess now. He knew that.

He had to believe that.

Taking a deep breath, he calmed himself enough to put the truck in gear. He was going to Dewey's Saloon and Steakhouse where he could get a beer or two, listen to country-and-western music and maybe talk to guys. Not confusing women. He rolled down the window, cranked up the stereo and accelerated when he hit the county road.

He'd been around Raven long enough that she had him asking questions about her day. About how she was feeling, for Cal's sake! He should never have quizzed her about what she was thinking. She got all mushy-eyed and said she missed her animals. Animals, always animals. What about people? She didn't have any problems assuming his great-grandparents had cared more about family than they had about the ranch—which was a big assumption—but she never talked about *her* family. She barely mentioned friends, But she had no qualms about chattering on about cattle, calves, rabbits, dogs, goats and cats.

Why was that? He wondered about her motives as the wind whipped through the truck cab and blew receipts and extra napkins off the seat. "Stop it," he told himself. He didn't want to think about why Raven wouldn't talk about her family when she was so interested in his. Her motives were none of his business. In a few days they'd get the mistake figured out, and she'd be gone. Off to research the heritage garden she'd been looking for, while he would *maybe* get some help from the consultant his brother had ordered.

He was better off getting help from Rodney and Burl. He kind of hoped that the mistake had been one-sided and his expert wouldn't show up.

He slowed as he neared town, then turned right at the abandoned mobile home that had been Brody's Crossing's one and only scandalous abode—a "massage parlor" from the 1980s that had aluminum foil on the windows. Patsy Klotsky, the proprietor, had always claimed it was because of the Texas heat and sunlight. His mother had made him look away as they'd driven past the old trailer. Now it was empty, overgrown with weeds and Johnson grass.

There were a lot of abandoned things in Brody's Crossing, and not all of them had foundations or wheels.

He shook off his dark thoughts as he made the next turn. In the distance, he saw the red, white and blue lights of Dewey's sign. Cowboys and ranchers hung out there, but they had a mind-set more like Cal's. He liked what Rodney and Burl had had to say this afternoon. Their advice to specialize, to stop competing against all the other big outfits, was sound. He'd already done some research on the Internet. Now he had to decide which breed and what market he needed to target.

If he'd had the money, he'd suggest the breed he

promoted. Unless he could get a grant, though, he knew Devborans were too expensive for the Rocking C. The strain was new and breeding stock limited. He'd need some truly innovative financing to pull that one off, and the Rocking C was already so far into the bank Cal would probably never get in the black.

As he shoved the truck into Park, he vowed to put thoughts of the ranch in the back of his mind. He was going to drink a couple of beers, have a good time, maybe play a little pool. Hang out with guys, who didn't make comments about family and heritage and fluffy pet animals.

Chapter Seven

The next morning Troy made himself a cup of coffee before he went to the barn to feed the animals. Raven was sound asleep and he wasn't about to wake her. He couldn't face her yet this morning. No matter how much beer he drank, it was hard to forget her soft, dark, sympathetic eyes or her need to care about everything around her. He didn't want to be one of those "things" she cared about.

His head ached and his stomach protested against the strong, acidic coffee he sipped on the way to the barn, but he was determined to make himself feel more human. He hadn't drunk too much at Dewey's since he had to drive home, but unfortunately, he'd carried on drinking when he got back to the ranch. Unable to sleep, he'd sat on the porch steps and watched the night sky, seeking some sort of cosmic answer to his problems.

He still didn't know what to do about the ranch, but he was working on it.

He fed the calves and let them out into their pen. They'd really grown in the past week. Soon he'd turn them out with the herd. Since they'd no longer be around the barn, Raven wouldn't fret about them. If she was still here. She might be gone by Monday, but he had a gut feeling she wouldn't.

He finished the morning chores and was just about to return to the house when he realized he wasn't alone. He turned to find her standing in the barn doorway, arms folded over a long sweater. Was she wearing a nightgown underneath, or was that another swirly-girly skirt? "You're not dressed for chores," he commented, closing the feed-room door.

"I wondered if you were home. When I went to sleep last night, you were gone, and when I woke up, you'd already made coffee and left."

"Worried about me?" he said as he walked toward her, dusting his hands off on his jeans.

"No, I was just curious." She glanced down at the dirt floor of the barn. "Well, maybe a little."

"I didn't drink too much and drive, if that's what you were concerned about."

"No, I didn't assume you would." She paused, then said, "I'm sorry if I said anything that I shouldn't have. Last night, that is. Sometimes I get too nosy. I hope you didn't leave the house on my account."

He stopped right in front of her. This was the tricky part, the part he didn't like. But it was for her own good. He'd decided, and he just needed to do it. "I'm a big boy, sweetheart. You don't need to mother me."

"I'm not mothering you," she said, frowning as she looked up at him.

"You mother everything. You're the consummate Earth Mother, you know that?" When she looked away, he tipped her chin up. Her eyes went wide open and surprised.

"What are you doing?"

"What do you think I'm doing?"

"I think you're flirting with me."

"Darlin'," he drawled, "if I was flirting with you, you wouldn't be thinking so hard about it. You'd know."

"I don't know *you*. Or why you're acting this way."

He had started out acting, but with her standing so close, smelling all feminine and morning-soft, he didn't have to pretend very much to give her the idea he wanted her. "Maybe it finally occurred to me that we're both healthy, single adults. If we're attracted to each other, why shouldn't we—"

"We shouldn't," she said, taking a pace back. She tripped on the wooden threshold and he reached out to steady her.

"Be careful. You'll fall and mess up your girly clothes."

"I'm fine. I'm going…I'm going back to the house. I'll fix breakfast, then I have a very busy day. Are you going to look for records of the old garden?"

He dropped his hands from her arms. "Sure I will." He gave her his best sexy-cowboy grin. "You let me know if you want to put off any of that busy day, now, you hear?"

She stepped out of the barn and backed up some more. "Yes, I hear you, but as I said, I have my day all planned." Then she turned and almost ran back to the house.

Troy let out a big sigh. Mission accomplished. She was scared of him. Maybe now she'd leave him alone. She'd leave the family history in the past, where it belonged.

RAVEN SPLASHED COLD WATER on her face, then blotted her skin dry and stared into the mirror. She looked as if she'd been hit by one of those horrible stun guns they used on cattle. She was surprised her naturally curly hair wasn't frizzed out all over her head.

What had happened to Troy? He'd come on to her as if she was trying to get picked up at a bar! All she'd done was express some concern and suddenly he was right in front of her, in full-out manly, invading-your-space mode. She knew the signs, although she rarely put herself in a situation where she'd be approached by a man on the prowl.

Troy must have gotten confused because he went out last night. Other than the one time they'd gone into town together for dinner, she didn't believe he'd gone out while she was here. And he'd been drinking, even if he hadn't been drunk when he drove home. She noticed the bottles in the trash when she'd gone into the kitchen.

Maybe that was it. Maybe he'd drunk too many beers at the house late last night and he was still slightly tipsy. Yes, that made perfect sense. It took hours for alcohol to leave the bloodstream. She'd read an article one time that said many people were still over the limit when they drove to work the next morning after a late-night drinking session.

Troy was still drunk, which is why he'd flirted with her. Which wasn't the least bit flattering. Suddenly, instead of shock, she felt disappointment. Was she only attractive to him when he'd had a couple of beers?

"Oh, what difference does it make?" she whispered as she dabbed a little salve on her lips. She didn't want him to find her attractive. She preferred not to think of him as an eligible, one-hundred-percent male. She just wanted a place to stay, a garden to document and credit for her work from the heritage garden society. If Mrs. Philpot ever got back to her office.

With a sigh, Raven left the refuge of her bathroom. She'd promised breakfast. Maybe some hearty food and more coffee would sober Troy up. So she wouldn't embarrass him about his lapse of judgment, she vowed that she would never bring up the subject.

As far as she was concerned, the incident was closed. Old news. Not important.

But oh, for a moment, he'd sure made her heart beat faster.

AFTER A BREAKFAST OF SCRAMBLED eggs, but no bacon, and great toast—he had to admit that Raven sure knew her bread—he pulled down the folding stairs to the attic. He wasn't sure much remained of his great-grandparents' possessions, much less his great-great-grandparents' things, but he'd promised that he'd look.

After scaring Raven this morning, it was the least he could do. Besides, staying busy with the garden and old papers would keep her from getting involved with the ranch. She might even stop bugging him about the calves.

He lost track of time as he went through the very oldest boxes and trunks. They were dusty and covered with cobwebs but were still where he remembered his mother showing him, many years ago. His father, for all his pride in the ranch, hadn't cared too much about family artifacts.

Maybe Raven knew a little more about his ancestors than he'd allowed last night. Not that he was going to divulge this recent revelation. She didn't need encouragement to become more involved, more sympathetic.

Again, he recalled how he'd pegged her the first day—she was too softhearted to survive on a ranch. Too empathetic for her own good.

There he was, thinking about Raven again. Reaching for the trunk, he pulled himself back to the task at hand—finding something to keep her occupied until she left to fix the real heritage garden. Soon he had several boxes and a trunk to bring downstairs.

After he'd moved all the cartons from the far end of the

attic, he noticed something he hadn't thought of since he was a boy. His great-grandmother's spinning wheel stood upright in the shadows, dusty yet proud. Funny, but he had forgotten the stories his grandmother told about the family, forgotten them completely until he'd seen all these old things up here.

He realized that he would now come face-to-face with his past in a whole different way—through the eyes of a New Hampshire outsider. He'd hope to give her something to keep her busy. But now he realized that what he was providing her would require answers. And that would mean dredging up his own past, his own memories.

With a groan, he grabbed each end of the one box and carried it toward the opening.

"Can I help?" Raven called up to him.

"It's kind of heavy." He was surprised she was talking to him already.

"I can handle it, I think."

He lowered the first box, then another. When it came time for the trunk, though, he climbed down the steps. "It's too heavy for you to manage alone," he told her as they carried it together down to the floor.

"This probably has the oldest records in it," he said. "There's no telling what you might find."

"Thank you," she said softly, not looking him in the eye, "for getting the boxes and trunk and also for trusting me to look through your family history."

"Not a problem. No one in the family is interested in it anyway. I'm sure you'll be bored to tears."

"Probably not. I love old things."

He carried the trunk into the guest bedroom and put it under the window so she could go through it at her own pace. "Let me know if you need anything, although I have to tell you that I don't know much about our history."

"I may ask you for names and dates."

"I'll do my best."

"Well, that's all I can hope for." She clasped her hands and looked down at the floor. "Are you feeling better now?"

"Better than what?"

"Than you were earlier this morning."

He stepped into the hall and grabbed a box. "Why did you think I wasn't well? I thought I was feeling pretty good."

"I...I just assumed that you'd been drinking last night and were perhaps still a bit tipsy."

"Now, why would you think that?"

"Oh, never mind. I just want to forget it."

"*It* being what happened in the barn, darlin'?"

"Yes. Of course." She folded her arms and glared at him.

He put the box down next to the trunk, then straightened and looked right at her. "Good luck with that," he said, again assuming his cowboy-lothario persona and giving her a lopsided grin.

Her mouth closed, her lips thinned and her eyes narrowed. "You're still drunk, aren't you?"

He chuckled, turned and shook his head. He'd really been convincing. Let his hippie houseguest think whatever she wanted. As long as she stopped getting all sentimental and mushy, he'd be fine.

RAVEN SPENT MUCH OF THE DAY at the old homestead with Riley and her digital camera. She documented everything, from the placement of the boards, to the weeds and plants as they existed now. She brought a ruler she'd found in the study to measure the plants she shot. When she was finished, she went back to the house, took a shower and changed from her jeans into a skirt and peasant blouse, and left Riley at the house. She drove into town, parking in front of the drugstore.

"Can you print photos here?" she asked the clerk.

"We can send the memory card out, or you can drive to Graham. They have a one-hour place there."

She drove to Graham. It wasn't that far, and she was surprised to find many more businesses and homes than in Brody's Crossing. At the drugstore she uploaded her photos, ordered double prints, then went to the largest grocery store to look for organic foods.

An hour later, her supplies boosted by the supermarket's adequate, if not impressive, selection, she picked up her pictures of the old homestead and drove home. No, not home. Back to the ranch. As Troy had pointed out, it wasn't his home, and it certainly wasn't hers. She was there temporarily, and if Mrs. Philpot got back in the office on Monday and discovered where Raven was supposed to be, she might be here two more days max.

But, just in case she wasn't sent off anywhere else, the Crawford-family garden had lots of potential. She didn't yet know what plants she'd discovered, but she would soon.

On the way back to the ranch, she stopped at the café for a cup of tea and one of their homemade sugar cookies. The owner had promised her he didn't bake with any hydrogenated oils or additives when she asked the other day, just in case she ever craved a cookie. Of course, she'd never tell Troy, but she had a sweet tooth that sometimes couldn't be satisfied with goat's-milk ice cream or honey-sesame squares. If he knew about that little weakness, he'd tease her even more.

Or, if he drank beer again and got into one of those weird, flirty moods, he might make even more suggestive comments. Not that she would welcome those, either. No, she was better off avoiding Troy as much as possible for the remainder of her stay. Perhaps she'd make a list of questions about his ancestors and slip it under the office door.

THE NEXT DAY RAVEN THREW herself into researching the plants she'd found at the old homestead. She used a few books she'd brought with her and the Internet on the Crawford computer, while Troy was working during the day. By Friday afternoon, she had identified several of the herbs, some peppers, a shrub and daffodil and grape hyacinth bulbs. She wrote a letter, included the photos, and took it all to the little post office inside the hardware store. Mrs. Philpot might not get it by Monday, but the documentation would arrive soon enough, so Raven would know in a few days whether she'd be staying in Texas or returning home to New Hampshire.

She and Troy had avoided each other fairly well. She'd seen him come into the house once, and another time she'd run into him in the hallway after his shower. That had been a close call. He hadn't said anything, just stared at her, and she'd apologized and perhaps stammered a bit before going into her room to fan her cheeks and calm her racing heart. Troy Crawford in jeans, a western shirt and boots was one thing; all damp and smelling good, towel around his neck and wearing nothing but jeans—that was enough to make her pulse skip a beat.

But at least he hadn't flirted with her. Of course, he hadn't been drinking. What a dismal thought—that she was only attractive to him when he'd had a beer.

When she arrived back at the ranch from her trip to town, he was preparing bottles for the calves' late-afternoon feeding. "May I help?" she asked for maybe the tenth time. He always said no.

"No, you can't feed the calves."

"I'm just trying to help."

"Then why not ask to muck out the horses' stalls?"

"I'm trying to be helpful, not self-abusive."

Troy laughed. "You can give the horses some oats and sweet feed. Their stalls don't need to be cleaned out anyway. They've been in the pasture."

"You've been riding a lot."

"All of us have been riding a lot. There's a ton of work to do, and my butt's not happy about it, either."

"Can I ride with you this weekend?"

"You ride?"

"English. I don't think I've ever ridden Western, except once on a pony at a little traveling circus. I think it had a saddle with a horn."

"I'm sure sitting in a bigger saddle is easier than balancing on one of those little pieces of leather."

"I have no idea, but I'd like to try."

"Sunday, then. I'm going to start separating the herd tomorrow. The regular hands will be here, plus a few extra cowboys from other ranches are coming over."

"Oh. I don't suppose I could help with that."

"No, you can't. You'd probably sort them by how pretty you think they are, and give each of them names."

She decided to ignore that last comment, but asked him again, just to be irritating, "Are you sure I can't feed the calves?"

"Yes, I'm sure. Stop asking me."

"Okay, I'll go see to the horses." She wasn't surprised that he didn't want her near those sweet little calves. She went out and scratched their little curly-hair heads and talked to them when Troy wasn't around. They were too cute. She hoped they would remain around the barn for a long time. But what if she had to leave? What would happen to them then? She knew, and she didn't want to think about it. She'd start crying again.

ON SATURDAY TROY WORKED with Cal's regular hands and two cowboys from a neighboring spread. They used the cutting horses to separate the cows with calves from the heifers, then moved all the beef cattle into another pasture. By the time he returned to the house around four o'clock, he was hot, tired, thirsty and hungry. And he didn't want to face his own cooking or more of Raven's whole wheat pasta, goat cheese and tofu.

He wanted a steak. A big, juicy, medium-rare T-bone.

Raven was busy on the computer, so he took a shower, shaved and splashed on a little cologne. He needed a haircut and his nails had seen better days. He'd developed calluses on his hands and probably his butt, but he hadn't been this fit in years. Working all day was a lot different than traveling, wining and dining prospective cattle buyers and attending stock shows. He no longer needed his upscale gym membership to stay in shape.

After he dressed in jeans and a plaid, western-cut shirt, he went to find Raven, to tell her what he was going to do. She was in the kitchen, chopping up something green and pungent.

"I'm off to Dewey's Saloon and Steakhouse for dinner." He watched her turn to him and tried his best to read her expression. She seemed a little disappointed. Damn. He'd been a bit hard on her lately, and he didn't like leaving her here alone. "I know it's not your usual kind of place, but would you like to go?"

"I'm not eating steak."

"They have salads and baked potatoes."

"Are you sure you want me to come?"

"I wouldn't have asked you if I didn't."

"This isn't some kind of date, is it? I mean, you might be drinking beer again, and I don't want you to—"

"I promise to be on my best behavior."

She considered his promise for a moment, her head turned slightly and her dark eyes searching. He guessed that he passed her mental lie-detector test. "In that case, I'd love to go."

"Okay, then. If you want to get ready, I'll put this back in the refrigerator for you."

She seemed surprised. "Thank you. I'll have it tomorrow instead."

He looked at the assortment of green things and wondered what they were and how she would fix them, then decided he didn't really want to know. She'd probably invite him to join her, and he wasn't sure his body was up to such a large quantity of organic, preservative-free, healthy stuff. Besides, she'd just mess it up with goat cheese and tofu.

By the time he'd cleaned up the kitchen, Raven was back and ready to go. She went over to the dog, leaned down and spoke to him as if he could understand. "We're going out for dinner, Riley. You stay here and take care of the house, and try to eat more of your dog chow. We'll be home soon."

While Troy enjoyed the sight of Raven's nicely rounded hips beneath the rather thin and clingy fabric of another one of her flouncy skirts, he couldn't believe she was talking to a dog. And advising him to eat that soybean crud she'd bought at the feed store. What were they thinking, carrying that stuff? It smelled funny and Riley didn't like it. Tonight, he vowed silently, he'd bring the dog back a real treat.

"Ready?" Raven asked, popping up from petting the dog.

"I'm ready." Ready to get out of this house and have a decent meal, cooked by someone who appreciates real food, and have a laugh for a change. How long had it been since he'd enjoyed going out? His most recent excursion to Dewey's had been fueled by frustration and anger. Tonight, he just wanted a good dinner and a little fun.

Wearing dainty canvas ballet slipper-type shoes, Raven walked toward the ranch pickup, but Troy stopped her. "I'm tired of driving the pickup. Let's take my car."

Chapter Eight

"Oh." She hadn't realized he had another car. It never occurred to her how he'd gotten here from wherever he lived. It seemed as if Troy had always been at the ranch because that's the only place she'd known him.

He steered her toward the garage and opened the creaking overhead door. A slightly dusty, big, silver SUV was parked in the hot, dark space. "Just wait outside and I'll start her up. It's kind of tight in here."

She stood and listened to the big engine, thinking of all the gallons of gas it must consume. Of course, it was impressive, she thought as he drove out of the garage. She hurried to the passenger side, and he leaned over and opened the door for her.

"Thanks. This is…surprising."

"That I own something that doesn't smell like cows, feed and manure?"

She ran her hands over the soft gray leather and looked at all the gauges and screens. This vehicle must be fitted with every device known to man. Compared to Pickles, this was as advanced as a spacecraft. Mind you, it probably didn't have a *name*. "I just hadn't thought about you having another life, that's all. To me, you're Troy Crawford of the Rocking C ranch. It's like you grew up here and never left, even though I know you did."

"I've only been back a few times. After I graduated from college. When my father died. Once, when Cal had his appendix out, I came back to take care of things for a week or so. But mostly, I've lived in Fort Worth."

"That's not very far, is it?"

"Not so much in miles, darlin'," he said, and accelerated as he pulled onto the county road. He reached over and turned the radio to a country-and-western station, stopping any further conversation about his life.

Raven settled back and tried to enjoy the scenery. They headed to town, then took a right and drove down another road. Before long she saw a red, white and blue sign proclaiming Dewey's Saloon and Steakhouse.

"Stay put," he said as he parked, switched off the engine and reached for his door.

He went around to her side and helped her out of the SUV, although she was perfectly capable of getting down by herself. "Thank you. If I didn't know better, I'd say you were treating me like a date, rather than an unwanted houseguest."

"Who said you were unwanted?"

She gave him a look that she hoped said, *Maybe you.*

"I told you the other night that I kind of liked having you around."

"I know you did," she confessed. "I just feel as if I'm imposing on you." Even if she had been trying to earn her keep by cleaning and cooking for him.

"It's not like that. Now, stop worrying and promise me you'll have a good time."

"I'll try."

"Okay, then."

They walked toward the front doors, which looked as if they belonged on a barn. The smell of cigarette smoke and beer rolled out, nearly making Raven gag. "You'll get used to it," Troy said as he pushed her through.

The decor wasn't any more inviting inside. There was a bar and dance floor to one side and a restaurant at the other. The head of a poor, dead longhorn hung over the bar, and in the restaurant, there were many horns of various sizes decorating the walls.

"Thank goodness there aren't any heads in here," she said as she followed Troy toward a table.

He ordered beer, and the waitress looked expectantly at her. "Do you have a microbrewed light ale?"

The waitress looked at Troy, who shrugged. "We've got Shiner, Bud and Miller Light on tap. Coors and Corona in bottles."

"Try a Shiner," Troy suggested. "It's from Texas."

She almost ordered a Coors just to be contrary. Why did Troy think all things Texan were better? "That will be fine."

"I didn't know you drank beer."

"I have nothing against alcohol. I just think it should be made—"

"As naturally as possible," Troy finished. "I know."

Raven smiled and spread her paper napkin in her lap. "I guess I am fairly predictable."

"And determined."

She shrugged. "When I believe in something, I can't help but act on it, one hundred percent."

"I know that about you." He leaned forward, so close she smelled his aftershave and his minty toothpaste. "But tonight, let's just have a good time."

"I'll do my best," she promised, settling back in her chair, away from temptation with a capital *T*.

The waitress returned with their beers. "To living in harmony," Troy toasted with his Bud longneck.

Raven clinked her glass against his bottle. *Maybe the beer will help,* she thought, glancing once more at the horns and antlers mounted on the wall.

After they ordered—she chose a salad, baked potato and a side order of mixed vegetables—she took another long drink of her Shiner and decided the night was going pretty well. At least, she thought so, since she'd never before been out with a single, eligible bachelor when it wasn't a date.

"Why don't you talk about yourself?" she asked Troy.

"You mean, like just start chatting right now?"

"No, I mean in general."

"I talk about myself. While we were driving over here, I told you about all the times I'd been back to the ranch."

"Yes, you did, but when I asked you about living in Fort Worth, you turned on the radio and tuned me out."

"Living in Fort Worth isn't all that interesting."

"Isn't that for me to decide? I'm from New Hampshire. I might find Fort Worth fascinating. I might even find your life interesting, if only you'd tell me about it."

"Why do you want to know, Raven? It's not like we have a lot in common and could compare notes. I travel, I go to rodeos and stock shows, I wine and dine ranchers. I don't see the attraction, unless you like cattle."

Maybe I like you, just a little, when you aren't being dictatorial and presumptive, she thought. But she didn't want to think about why she found Troy interesting when she hated cattle ranching.

"I'm sorry. I've probably hurt your feelings again. I didn't mean to. I just meant that my job is to promote something that you believe is wrong. It doesn't mean I'm right. It just means that you and I have different lives. I imagine yours is more interesting than mine, to tell you the truth, but I'm not sure because you don't talk about yourself much, either."

"I don't?"

"No, you don't. I know about your beliefs, your animals, and a little bit about your state. But nothing about you."

She sat back in her chair. She'd never considered what he was saying. Was he right? "What do you want to know?"

He smiled and shook his head. "Hell, I don't know. I was just saying that before you criticize me, you might think about how little you give away."

"I don't mind talking about myself." She took another drink of her beer. "But really, Troy, I don't remember you asking."

He sat back in his chair and drained his bottle. "You might be right. Most of the time, I've been so caught up in my brother's mess that I've been poor company. I've been an even worse host."

"No, you haven't. Well, except that one time when you upset me. And maybe that time when you were drunk."

"I've never been drunk around you!"

"I meant, you'd been drinking and were obviously still feeling the effects when you started flirting with me."

"Raven, I wasn't drunk."

"I really think it's the most logical conclusion."

He leaned back again and smiled, looking rather surprised and amused. "You really want to believe that, don't you?"

She was saved from answering by the arrival of their

salads. As she drizzled vinegar and oil over the lettuce and mixed greens, she wondered why Troy was claiming he wasn't tipsy when he'd come on to her. But if he hadn't been drinking, then why? Why had he suddenly found her so attractive?

She didn't understand him. And she definitely didn't want to talk about that incident anymore. "So how long have you lived in Fort Worth?" she asked, changing the subject as effectively—she hoped—as he'd switched direction on her more than once.

TROY FELT A LOT BETTER AFTER two beers, a salad, a big ol' steak and loaded baked potato. He passed on dessert and, instead, asked the waitress to hold their table. And, when Raven wasn't listening, told her to wrap up the steak bone in a doggy bag.

"Let's dance," he said to Raven as she tapped her fingers on the table in time to the music drifting in from the bar area.

"Oh, I don't know country-and-western dances."

"Don't worry. I'll show you." He reached for her hand and pulled her gently from the chair. "You can't come to Texas and not two-step."

"I believe I could."

"What would be the fun of that? You look pretty fit. I'll bet you can dance."

"Well, a little, but—"

"No more excuses. I'm going to show you how to Texas two-step, and if they play the right music, I might even teach you the Cotton-Eyed Joe."

"Be still my heart," she murmured as he led her to the worn parquet dance floor.

"You'll be fine. Just follow my lead."

He found a space on the edge of the floor and positioned himself in front of Raven. "This is a really simple step. We'll go slow at first."

"It might be a good idea to go slow, period."

He held her right hand in his, then took her left and put it on his shoulder. They stood less than a foot apart, and he smelled her floral fragrance and sensed her heat. He put his right arm around her waist, then leaned close. "Oh, I can go slow, darlin'."

She looked up at him, all wide-eyed wonder with a touch of apprehension. He grinned and pulled her a little nearer, so he could guide her to the music. "Remember, I'm leading," he said.

He stepped forward and when she didn't move at first, their bodies bumped together. She jumped back, and he pulled her in again. "Relax."

"Easy to say. You know how to dance."

"You will, too, in a little while."

Once she loosened up, the two-step went easier. He left her after the second song to ask something of the band. The next tune was nice and slow, and when Raven began to relax, he pulled her a little closer.

"You can feel the music better this way," he said, but knew that was only an excuse to feel her lithe body and firm breasts against him. He was playing with fire. He shouldn't be thinking of Raven in a sexual way unless he planned to take their relationship to the next level. He wasn't. She would be gone sooner or later. He didn't need complications of any kind when the situation at the ranch was so unsettled.

He'd learned the hard way, from having two former girlfriends over the past five years or so, that no matter what consenting adults said about keeping a relationship simple, without commitment and just for fun, things always went wrong.

Once, he'd gotten a little serious with a girlfriend. He started thinking about the future. They were comfortable together, and he thought maybe they could be just like that, forever. Regular sex and enjoyable dinners with no drama. She, however, had loved her career and liked the fact that he was gone a lot. It made the sex better, she claimed, and allowed them to be at ease with each other because there was no future. He'd tried it, but it hadn't worked for him. He resented her for not wanting anything else when he'd started thinking he might.

And then the opposite happened with his next partner. He'd vowed to keep things light and simple, while she'd started getting serious. She wanted to come with him sometimes when he traveled. She invited him to spend Thanksgiving with her parents in Arizona. When he tried to pull back, she tried to talk about their feelings for each other. He'd gotten out of that relationship before things got really messy.

So, he knew that even if he and Raven were two mature people living in the same house, they had too many differences and there was too much potential for heartache. The sex would be good, but she'd either leave before they got bored, in which case they might make the disastrous decision to continue the relationship, or they might tire of each other while she was still here, which would be worse.

No, it wasn't worth it. He could control himself, even if he hadn't had sex in months and he found her more than attractive, despite her lectures and their opposing beliefs.

"Let's sit this one out," he said as the band began a new, livelier number. "I could use another beer."

RAVEN WAS GRATEFUL FOR THE break from dancing. She'd enjoyed being held in Troy's arms and guided around the floor more than she liked to admit. Troy had felt warm and solid beneath her fingers, and smelled too good to ignore. She ordered another beer and settled back in her chair as her breathing returned to normal.

"Is this your usual hangout?" she asked while they waited for their drinks.

"No, not really. I've been too busy to socialize, and it's not that great coming alone."

She smiled to herself, glad that he was having fun with her. Of course, that was a very foolish thing to be glad about. His happiness wasn't her responsibility, and hers shouldn't depend on having a good time at a Texas honky-tonk.

The beers arrived, and they drank in silence for maybe a minute. Troy turned to her and said, "Thanks for coming with me tonight."

"You're welcome."

They took another sip, then as if he were a little boy who couldn't keep his attention on one thing very long, he turned to the bar area. "Come on. They've announced they're going to play 'Cotton-Eyed Joe.' You have to learn how to dance that while you're in Texas."

"Really, the two-step was enough."

"Nonsense," he said, standing up and pulling her to her feet. "Quick. You can get all the steps down pat before the music really picks up."

Raven groaned, but he ignored her and dragged her onto the dance floor again. She had liked dancing the two-step in Troy's arms, but had a feeling she was going to regret this rousing Cotton-Eyed Joe.

"WHAT ARE YOU LAUGHING ABOUT?" Raven asked as they drove back to the ranch.

"That shoe. The look on Bud Hammer's face when it whacked him up the side of his head." Troy chuckled and tried to keep from bursting into full-out laugh mode. He might just have to pull the SUV off the road if he couldn't control himself.

"I swear, I had no idea my shoe would fly off my foot like that."

"I'll say this for you. You have a hell of a kick."

"You told me to kick!"

"Not like a mule!" He started laughing again.

Raven went silent, and when he glanced over, her arms were folded over her chest. "Oh, come on. It was funny. And I didn't mean you kicked like a mean ol' ornery mule. More like a cute, pretty little mule."

"Oh, that makes it so much better."

He stifled another guffaw and reached over to tug at her hand. "Come on, don't be mad. Or embarrassed. It was hilarious."

"Bud didn't think so. I suppose he believes I did that on purpose."

"No, he doesn't. He just doesn't like to be laughed at. He's an ass. Don't pay any attention to him."

"He's your neighbor, isn't he?"

"But not a close one. And believe me, he hasn't given me any helpful advice on how to save the ranch."

"I've just never kicked off a shoe, had it arch across a room and hit someone in the head. The experience was rather…startling."

"More for Bud than for you."

"That's debatable." She pulled her hand away but

relaxed a little in the seat. "I'm just glad I was wearing something lightweight."

"Next time, wear your boots. They won't slide off your feet."

"Next time?"

"Sure. We had fun, didn't we?"

"Well, yes, we did."

"You sound surprised."

"I've never been to a saloon and steakhouse before, never danced country-and-western, never really done anything like that."

"Do you have to dwell on it that much? Either you had a good time or you didn't."

She was silent a moment, then said, "You're right. I'm overthinking again."

"Just relax. It was a great evening. You didn't violate any of your personal ethics. You didn't do anything dangerous. Well, except maybe to Bud, but next time you won't wear those slippery shoes."

"Okay, next time I'll be more careful."

"Terrific."

They were both silent for a while as they approached the turnoff to the ranch. He wondered what she was thinking, and then wondered why he was wondering. And that got him irritated that Raven was on his mind way too much. But they had had a good time tonight, which surprised him. He'd wondered if she was too uptight to have fun. When she didn't try to lead or think too hard about what she was doing, she was a darn good dancer, too.

"I'm making good progress on the old documents in the trunk and boxes," she said as he turned off the county road onto the driveway.

"Good. Find anything helpful?"

"There were some receipts and an old journal that mentioned planting. The entries didn't continue for very long, though. Tomorrow I'm going through a stack of letters that were written to someone, I guess your great-grandfather, while he was away. He must have returned the letters and they were saved. They're tied with a pink ribbon. I hope it's okay to look at them. I promise I'll just read the parts pertaining to the garden."

"I don't care if you read them all, Raven. There's nothing in the distant past that's worth hiding. At least, I've never been told there was the slightest scandal."

The only part of his history he didn't want to go into concerned his parents. His mother. He couldn't talk about what she'd done, probably because he'd never understood the why. How did a mother go off and leave her sons and her husband?

"I just wanted you to know that I'm only looking for information about the garden. Even though this isn't the one I'm supposed to be researching and restoring, I would love to save the plants. Isn't it amazing that they've survived all this time?"

"Yeah, I guess it is. I'm going to have to climb the hill and see this garden. To me, the old homestead always looked like a bunch of rotten lumber and weeds. My father always told us to stay away because it was dangerous."

"It can be. There are smashed dishes and glass, rusted nails and weathered broken boards that are nearly as hard as metal. It would be unsafe for children."

"I guess you've had your tetanus booster and all the other shots you might need, right?"

"Oh, yes. I handle a lot of metal on the farm, plus you never know what's buried just beneath the dirt. Artifacts work their way up through the soil, and suddenly there's part of a barrel rim, or a bucket handle, or glass shards. I don't want my animals stepping on those."

Of course she didn't. She probably cared more about them than she did herself. "If we scoured our pastures for dangerous items, we'd never get anything else done."

"That's why I have six acres and you have over a thousand."

He pulled the SUV up to the garage. "The Rocking C used to be bigger, but my father sold some of it off when I was still a kid. He sure wasn't happy to do it, but we had a drought and hay prices shot through the roof. We had to thin the herd and sell land. Cal swore he'd never do that again, but hell, that's exactly what should be done."

"Are there buyers?"

"I don't know. I haven't gotten that far, but I need to find out."

"How about people to lease the land? Could you do that?"

"I'm not sure."

She laid her hand on his arm. "I know you don't want to talk to me about the ranch, but I'd like to mention diversification again. You might be able to make more money if you didn't depend on only one…product."

"You mean beef."

"Well, whatever you end up growing or raising."

"You sound like an economist."

She shrugged. "I took some courses in college. It's good to know your options. That's one reason I raise goats, sheep and rabbits. I can harvest their wool and fur, sell the goats' milk and raise them as pets. I have different sources of income in case one market is weak."

He was surprised that they were now talking so rationally about his ranch problem. And, she was sort of talking about herself. Not as much as he'd like, but she was revealing a little.

"I'll take that into consideration." He smiled in the near darkness of the vehicle, lit only by the dashboard lights. "Maybe you should be a ranching consultant after all."

"Oh, no! I could never do that. I nearly cried when I drove up to the ranch the first time."

"I didn't know that," he said. But he wasn't surprised. She was the most softhearted woman he'd ever met. She was right—she wouldn't last ten minutes on most ranches. And she could never go to the Fort Worth Stockyards, which were maybe two miles from his condo.

He turned off the engine. "We'd better get inside. I imagine your mutt will be glad to see you."

"I'm sure Riley needs to go outside. We've been gone a long time."

Raven scooted out of the SUV before he could help her. At the last minute, Troy remembered the doggy bag he'd put behind the seat. Riley deserved a little treat after eating nothing but soy chow—and the occasional sneaky, leftover, late-night treat—for days.

Chapter Nine

Raven got busy on Sunday, sorting the receipts, journals and letters from the Crawford ancestors into stacks according to dates and subjects. She read the letters to Calvin P. Crawford from his wife, Minerva. They were mostly about their family and neighbors, but she also mentioned their crops and dishes she'd served at home or taken to ailing neighbors.

If she found the recipes, Raven could identify the herbs and other ingredients Minerva had used. She wondered if there were any old recipes or cookbooks in the house that might be pushed to the back of a cabinet or hidden away someplace that men never looked. Most older cooks had their favorites memorized, so unless Troy's great-grandmother had written them down for a daughter or daughter-in-law, they probably didn't exist.

Troy worked in the barn, then rode out in the afternoon. He had returned a little while ago and offered to take Riley with him while he cared for the horses. Raven felt a little surprised, but grateful for Riley's sake. That dog adored Troy.

She could sympathize. Troy was pretty adorable most

of the time. He'd been very agreeable, but not overly flirty,
since yesterday. Not that she'd seen him that much, since
they were both busy. But once or twice she'd caught him
looking at her in a considering way, as if he was trying to
figure something out. Maybe she'd made remarks last night
that made him think. If so, that was good. She wanted this
ranch to survive in some form, especially since, through
their written records, she'd come to know the Crawfords
who'd founded the place.

She'd also prefer the cattle to survive, which maybe
was asking too much. What could Troy do with a herd of
beef cattle? Sometimes, life was cruel. That didn't mean
she couldn't fight the obvious outcome or wish it were
different.

Late that afternoon, Troy came in dusty and tired with
a very happy Riley, his doggy grin brightening the kitchen.
While Troy showered, Raven fixed dinner—spaghetti with
tomato sauce. And for Troy's sake, she didn't even put
goat cheese in it. She placed bowls of salad and grated
Parmesan on the table, then spread toasted bread with
organic butter and garlic. Surely there was nothing about
this meal that Troy would find objectionable.

He dug in with a hearty appetite. "This is great," he
finally said, and Raven felt herself glowing at the compliment. She knew she and Troy had their differences, but she
was finally doing something constructive in Texas, and the
two of them had settled into a truce. A working relationship, she supposed. What else could she call their cohabi-
tation? Did they have enough in common to form a
friendship that would last beyond her return to New
Hampshire?

He offered to clean up the kitchen since she'd cooked,

but she'd been so bent over papers all day while he was working hard she insisted on doing it.

Troy settled into the living room to watch the hockey game. When she was finished with the kitchen, she came in and picked up her knitting. Riley lay at the foot of Troy's ottoman, obviously tired out.

"Thanks again for supper. It was good."

"You're welcome."

Raven settled back on the couch. The whole scene seemed so normal, so domestic, that she couldn't really believe what was happening. Days ago she'd felt alone and homesick while sitting on the couch like this. Now she was filled with a sense of peace and maybe the promise of good things to come. She didn't want to overthink this moment, but she couldn't help wondering whether these feelings were real, or just an illusion.

On Monday morning, Troy did his barn chores with the help of his new shadow, Riley, then grabbed a cup of Raven's coffee. "Who's fixing breakfast this morning?" he asked as he sipped the hot brew.

"I can. I was thinking of doing French toast."

"Really? That's...that sounds great." He paused on his way to the study. "You aren't going to put anything weird in it, are you?"

"No. I found some organic cow's milk when I went to Graham, so I can use that."

"Er, does that mean it's also unpasteurized? It might have germs."

"That's what the dairy industry wants you to think." He stared at her a moment, and she added, "Look, I'm using it, too. I wouldn't eat or drink anything that wasn't safe."

"Maybe."

"Trust me. I only want you to be healthy."

"I am healthy."

"You don't know that. You might feel much better and live longer if you ate a more natural diet."

"Darlin', if I felt any better, you wouldn't be able to stand me."

Raven rolled her eyes. "Laugh if you want. I know what I'm talking about."

Troy chuckled. "I'm looking forward to that French toast. I'll go check the e-mail. Maybe we've heard from someone."

"Oh, good idea. Let me know if they've sorted anything out."

He went into the study, sat behind the desk and turned on the computer. He looked at himself in the blank, dark monitor and realized he was grinning. Oh, that was wrong. He shouldn't let Raven make him smile, should he?

The computer booted up and Troy clicked on the Internet icon. His brother didn't pay for high-speed DSL so the modem whirled and groaned and dialed the service provider. This was way too slow. He should get a satellite link for his laptop. Just because he was stuck on a 1950s-style ranch didn't mean he had to endure outdated technology.

Finally, he accessed his e-mail. And there, from the rancher's association, was a reply. He opened it with mixed feelings. He needed the kind of help a consultant would provide, right? But if they had the mix-up straightened out, Raven might be gone by tonight.

And then who would care about his diet and his health?

"Come and get it," Raven called out in the direction of the study. The French toast was thick and golden. She'd put some local honey on the table because she didn't have pure maple syrup. She poured herself a small glass of milk, and poured Troy a larger one.

He came into the kitchen without making any mouthy comments, which must mean the French toast looked good.

They sat down and ate. She watched Troy taste the milk. He didn't groan or make a face. But he sure was quiet. "Was there an e-mail?"

"Yes, there was." He chewed and swallowed. "The French toast is great, by the way."

She put down her fork. "Troy, what did it say?"

"It seems that once upon a time a married couple managed the ranchers' and heritage garden associations. They did everything by hand, but at some point in the 1980s, they hired someone to create a database. Then the husband got sick and gave up running the Farmers' and Ranchers' Society while the wife, who was getting older, still hung on to the heritage garden society."

"Okay, but that was years ago. How did they scramble our assignments?"

"Apparently a long time ago, when my mother lived… here, she wrote to the garden society. She was interested in the old homestead. Apparently she had the same thing in mind that you did—identifying the plants and preserving them."

"Oh, that was lovely of her."

"Yeah, so anyway, her request for an expert was entered in the database before the groups broke apart completely. Each society got a copy of the old list. When my brother wrote in requesting a consultant be sent to the Rocking C, it was assumed that he was following up on the very old letter from our mother asking for help with the garden. The request was forwarded to your garden association, and voilà, here you are."

"Wow." She sat back in her chair and thought a moment. "So, there never was a cattle expert, was there?"

"No. Apparently, Cal thought it would just happen because this was the old reliable association my father had used."

"Oh, Troy. Don't be so hard on him. He couldn't have known about the merged database."

"No, I suppose not," he said, taking a deep breath. "I guess I'm just frustrated with him. I mean, he's so stubborn, just like our old man. It's like living here as a child again. It brings back a lot of old memories."

"I understand." She pushed her plate aside and put her hand on his. "I'm sorry you're not getting the professional advice you were expecting, but really, I think you have everything you need right here."

"What do you mean?"

"You have good friends, fellow ranchers. You have other resources, like the Internet. There are probably buddies outside Brody's Crossing that you can call upon." She paused when he continued to look at her. "And me, for what it's worth. I'll help you all I can."

"I know you will. I know I can rely on the others, too. But really, what the ranch needs and what Cal wants are two different things. If I make any changes, he'll try to put everything back as it was when he comes home. Then the place will be in even worse shape."

"If you did something really dramatic, he couldn't do anything."

"What are you talking about?"

"I mean that if he can't replace the cattle, if you've made financial commitments, then he'd just have to get used to it."

"I don't know, Raven. This ranch is his life."

"You keep saying you want to save the Rocking C. But how are you going to without doing something drastic?"

"I don't know. I'm thinking about it."

"Okay."

"I'm not dismissing your ideas. I'm not eliminating anything, including selling the whole place and starting over again. But I've got a few more things to research, to think about, before I make any decisions."

"Sure, but really, I don't think you should sell. There's a lot of history here. Your ancestors put so much of themselves into this land. I know they'd want you to keep it in the family."

"That's my goal." He pulled his hand away and looked down at his plate. "Now, let me finish this French toast. I swear, between the spaghetti last night and the breakfast this morning, you're getting to be a darn good cook."

AFTER BREAKFAST, TROY GOT TO WORK with the cowboys who were sorting the herd and doing whatever cowboys did. Raven wasn't sure, and didn't really want to know. Whatever they were up to probably caused either pain or distress to the cattle, and being unaware meant it couldn't haunt her later.

Using the phone in the office, she called Mrs. Philpot to figure out the details of the consultant she needed up in New Hampshire in June. Mrs. Philpot was amazed at the Texas mix-up and was eager to work with Raven, assuring her the society would reimburse her expenses while she worked on the Crawford garden. She told Mrs. Philpot to look for the packet she'd sent at the end of last week, then hung up with a smile on her face. The day was improving and it was time to celebrate. She let Riley go to the barn because he'd been so well behaved lately, and headed into town.

She knew her new friends had lunch every day at noon, so she headed for the café. She needed some time away from the ranch, away from Troy. He continued to confuse her. He could be cool one minute and warm the next. When he looked at her and smiled, when she touched him and he didn't pull away, she felt happy. But she knew that wasn't a good thing. She shouldn't allow herself to fall for someone who would not be in her life very long. But just as she reacted to animals in need, she wanted to help Troy. Sometimes he reminded her of a beast that had been hurt in some way and was reluctant to trust, or to allow affection.

She imagined that Troy Crawford found sex a lot easier to handle than any type of emotional intimacy.

Just another way in which they were the exact opposites.

She parked Pickles near the café and gathered her tote bag. She had a few herbal concoctions for Clarissa Bryant and Ida Bell. In return, she hoped they would help her with some ideas for relocating the Crawford garden or at least saving the plants she'd found. These were obviously hardy perennials and reseeding annuals. They'd withstood drought, heat and freezing temperatures for over a hundred years. She'd like to find a place for them, perhaps a mini heritage garden, right here in Brody's Crossing.

"How are you and Troy getting along?" Clarissa asked with a grin and a wink. "He's a tall drink of water, that one."

"Fairly well, considering we have hardly anything in common."

"I heard from Myrna Hammer that the two of you were cutting it up on the dance floor at Dewey's Saturday night."

"Well, I'm not sure how much we were 'cutting up,' but

we did have dinner there and Troy attempted to teach me some country-and-western dances."

"Myrna said the two of you looked like a real couple," Ida mentioned rather casually. "She also said you whacked Bud in the head with your shoe. Accidentally, of course."

"What Myrna probably meant was that she thinks more is going on at the Crawford ranch than just documenting plants and herding cattle." Clarissa added sweetener to her tea.

"There's not," Raven said emphatically. "I mean, he is very attractive, but as I said, we have nothing in common."

"Sometimes, that's best," Clarissa said. "My late husband, God bless his soul, was an accountant. He didn't like socializing and couldn't understand how I could 'gossip' all day long in the beauty shop. But we shared enough, I'll tell you that. He cared about my feelings and I never made him go out when he'd rather stay at home."

Ida nodded. "If you're too much alike, it gets dull."

"Exactly," Clarissa confirmed. "Believe me, you don't want dull. I hear about that all day long at the salon. Abusive men, boring men. Add a dose of ungrateful children, and you've got my day."

Raven smiled. "I understand what you're saying, but really, it has nothing to do with Troy and me. We're not an item."

"You could do worse," Clarissa advised.

"And Troy would be lucky to get you," Ida added. "You'd keep that boy jumping!"

Raven knew she affected Troy in some way, but she wasn't sure he'd consider her contribution to ranch life a good thing. More than likely, he'd rather brood in silence, amid the dreary beige of the run-down house. "I'll be leaving as soon as I finish the garden. And I'm not even sure how long Troy will be at the ranch. He's working awfully hard to update the Rocking C, although he's mentioned his brother won't like any changes."

"His brother needs to live in the present," Ida said, a frown on her face. "That boy was too close to his daddy. Everyone always said he was a chip off the old block. He took that to heart. He never left, like Troy did, to become his own person."

"He's certainly gone now, though. All the way to Afghanistan, risking his life." Clarissa shook her head. "I hope he comes home safe."

Their lunch arrived, and the topic, thankfully, shifted to herbs suitable for various ailments. Raven had a fascination for the Crawford family, but she would never let Clarissa or Ida know that. Any interest might be seen as encouragement, and these two ladies didn't need fuel for their fire. They obviously though that if a single man and a single woman were living in the same house, sparks would inevitably fly.

Sparks might be flying, but they weren't the romantic kind, Raven told herself. They were kindled by two opinionated individuals rubbing each other the wrong way. Of course, that didn't mean she and Troy didn't have moments when they got along fine. Like Saturday night. Eating dinner and dancing had been fun. Being in his arms had been even mildly exciting. Well, maybe more than mildly. But she wasn't going to dwell on her strictly physical attraction to a good-looking rancher.

"When you finish work on the homestead, we should have a party," Ida said. "I remember that Cal and Troy's mother used to work on that old garden. She mentioned it to me more than once."

"A party at Dewey's would be a good idea," Clarissa said. "You could meet more of the people around here."

"Oh, I'll probably be getting back to New Hampshire shortly. My friend, Della, is looking after my farm and taking care of my animals, but I'm sure she's getting tired of living my life. I have a business to run."

"And you have a very attractive cowboy down here," Clarissa said with an all-knowing smile.

"Really, Troy isn't my type."

"Oh? What kind of man do you like? Is there someone special back in New Hampshire?"

"No, no one special. I've dated some teachers and professors from nearby Manchester. I had a fairly long relationship with a yoga instructor there."

Clarissa and Ida looked at each other. "Gee, academic types and yogis! Nothing against them, girl, but compared to a cowboy?"

Raven smiled and shrugged. Okay, next to Troy, her former boyfriends didn't pass the "hunk" test, but they were comfortable. She shared beliefs with them. They talked about intellectual issues and she could eat meals with them without getting into the meat-versus-soy debate. If they weren't as physically appealing, at least they weren't dictatorial and intimidating. They didn't loom over her or invade her space. They didn't make her do things she didn't want to do.

She placed her chin in her palm and leaned on the table. "You're right. They're boring."

Her friends laughed and ordered dessert.

Chapter Ten

That night Troy came in a little early from his ranch work while the cowboys finished culling the steers. Troy needed to make a decision about which ones were going to market now, before he had to buy hay for the summer. Unfortunately, the Rocking C didn't have sufficient pasture to cut and bale. If the drought continued and feed prices remained high, it would be more cost-effective to sell the steers soon. Besides, the price of beef was up at the moment. He might as well take advantage of that.

Cal would probably have a cow, so to speak, when he learned that half the herd was gone, but that was the reality of the ranch. They needed money this month, not more expenses in the future.

He sat down behind the computer and got online—finally. He found the Web site for tracking the price of beef and compared it with other years by month. He started to print the page he wanted, but the printer was out of paper. Great. He didn't know where Cal kept his supplies, so he started hunting.

In the second drawer on the right, beneath some clipped-together flyers from various cattlemen's groups and upcoming stock shows, was a picture that Troy hadn't seen in nearly twenty years. He removed the old tarnished gold-tone frame and looked at the professional photo of himself, Cal and their mother. Man, they all looked so young! Cal was in high school, and Troy thought he'd been in ninth grade. Their mother would have been less than forty years old then. Her blond hair was shoulder length and curled, kind of layered away from her face. She looked...pretty.

She didn't look like a woman who was planning to desert her family.

The photo transported him back to when it had been taken. His mother had bought a portrait package at the Olan Mills Studio in Fort Worth and his father had pitched a fit. It was a waste of money, the old man had claimed. They had a camera, and regular photos were expensive enough. Those packages were just a rip-off to make you buy more.

His mother had stood firm, though, and said she wanted a picture with her boys. They'd left their father at the ranch, doing what he liked to do best, anyway, and drove to Fort Worth. They made a day of it, doing school shopping and having lunch. Troy remembered that his brother had been unusually quiet and fidgety, as if he was uncomfortable being that far away from the Rocking C. Troy had loved it all, though, except for the shopping.

He hadn't liked to try on different clothes then and still didn't. Nowadays he found a few basic pants and shirts that appealed and ordered them online in different colors. Of course, then there were suits. He had to venture into stores for those, of course, but thankfully, not too often. He really didn't understand the fascination with shopping.

His mother had enjoyed that day, though, he recalled as he rubbed the frame. She'd insisted her boys have nice new clothes. Had she known then that she'd be leaving and didn't want her sons to be ragged or wearing clothes they'd outgrown? Who knew? She never said she was unhappy, although she and his father had argued all the time. She'd never talked about leaving them.

One day, she'd just packed her suitcase and gone, while he and Cal had been at school and their father was off somewhere on the ranch. She'd left brief letters for himself and Cal. No final hugs. No kiss good-bye. No explanation.

How did a mother go off and leave her children? He hadn't understood then why or how she'd done that. He never would.

With a sigh, he placed the photo back in the drawer, on top of the ranching and stock-show brochures, and closed the drawer. All those memories. All those painful feelings he could usually keep under control.

And just because he'd wanted some printer paper.

BUOYED BY HER RECENT COOKING success and her realization that she would be staying in Brody's Crossing for at least another two weeks, Raven decided to do everything possible to help Troy succeed in his goal to save the ranch. It didn't seem fair that she would get what she needed—a heritage garden to restore—while he would get nothing. She would take over as many chores as possible, cook food he liked as long as it didn't involve meat and try her best to be cordial.

As for her physical attraction to him, that had to stop. She would be friendly but not flirty. Not that she'd ever come on to him. Troy was the one who'd stepped over the platonic bounds.

For supper she fixed black-bean "burgers," with pepper

jack cheese for him and goat cheese for her. She put them on whole wheat buns and provided a platter of leaf lettuce, sliced tomatoes and onions. While Troy showered, she set the table and made iced green tea.

"Wow, this looks good," he said when he entered the kitchen. "Are those real burgers?"

"Of course not. But I think you'll like them."

He did, eating two. "You know," he said as he finished his meal, "maybe there is something to this healthy-eating plan of yours. I have to admit, I feel better than I did last week or the week before."

"I'm glad. You're working so hard and I want to help."

"Coming home to a meal is a nice bonus, but you don't have to do that. I know you're going to be busy on the garden."

"I'm going to try to work outside during the cooler morning hours. Then in the afternoon, I'll do research and paperwork. I'll still have plenty of time to give you a hand."

"Do you have something specific in mind?"

"Oh, just whatever you think I could handle."

His eyes narrowed. "Are you talking again about feeding those calves?"

"I...I had thought about that. And the horses, of course. And the chickens—gathering eggs and feeding them."

He pushed his plate back and leaned forward on his forearms. "You know how I feel about you looking after those calves. You'll get attached to them. I guarantee it."

"I'll consider it a job. They're your calves, not mine."

"Actually, they're Rocking C calves."

"I'll take good care of them, though. Just like they were my own, only they're not."

Troy shook his head. "Something tells me this is not a great idea."

"I'm just trying to help."

He threw both hands up in surrender. "Okay, you can feed Hamburger, Tenderloin and Prime Rib."

"What?"

"The calves. I've named them. Every time you look at them, I want you to remember that they're beef cattle."

"That's horrible!"

"I'm serious, Raven. These are not pets. They're joining the herd as soon as I have the cattle sorted and know which ones that are going to stay, and which are…leaving."

"You're selling some stock?"

"Well, I'm selling some of the cattle. I've decided that now is the best time, with beef prices fairly high and the cost of hay bound to rise during the summer."

She felt distress all through her body, just as she had the first time she'd seen the cows' white faces and stocky red bodies as they grazed in the pasture. "But this is their home," she said without thinking.

"Raven, don't start this."

She closed her eyes and took a deep breath. "You're right. I'm sorry. They're Rocking C cattle."

"That's right. I'm doing what's best to save this ranch for whatever purpose I decide on. It makes more sense to get rid of the excess stock now, before I have to go into even more debt buying hay for the summer."

She held up her hand. "No, you're right. I'm not used to ranching in Texas. I don't have any idea about the cost of hay."

"Right. You remember that while you're looking after Hamburger, Tenderloin and Prime Rib." He got up from the table. "Thanks again for supper. It was great."

She squeezed her eyes shut and swallowed the lump in her throat. Somehow she would find a way to save those calves, if she had to dress them up in sheep's clothing and tell Troy her new pets' names were Woolly, Fleecy and Lamb Chop. The hand puppet, not the meat.

TROY AND RAVEN KEPT BUSY. She fed the barn animals, collected eggs from the chickens and fretted over the calves. As per Troy's instructions, she was weaning them from the bottle and feeding them a little grain. She let them out all day in their enclosure so they could graze. So they would be ready to join the herd. Every time she watched their big brown eyes through the fence, she nearly cried.

"I won't let him kill you," she promised them, but didn't know how she'd keep it. She couldn't afford to buy three calves, and what would she do with them if she did? They didn't belong on her New Hampshire farm. They took up too much room and caring for them for the next twenty years or so would cost her a fortune. If she sold them to another farmer or rancher, she couldn't be certain that they'd be safe forever, especially during hard times.

Riley nudged her hand, seeming to commiserate. He'd become a fairly good "calf" dog by helping her move the animals out of their stall into the enclosure. Maybe someday he'd be a good cow dog. If he stayed on the ranch. She wasn't sure what she would do about Riley any more than she knew what she'd do about those calves.

After early-morning chores, she worked on the garden. In two days she'd carefully cleared most of the fallen lumber and dangerous broken chards and rusted metal. She'd uncovered mustard greens, dill and some other herbs that were barely peeking through the dirt and debris.

On a broken fence grew the tangled mess of a climbing rose. She wanted to prune it, but it was the wrong time of year. The best she could do was cut away the dead branches and try to start some new plants from judicious cuttings. She probably wouldn't be here long enough to see if they rooted, but if the main plant flowered in the next week or so, she could send photos to the heritage garden society to have it identified. If it wasn't already registered, then she could apply to the heritage rose associations to have it recognized as a new variety.

Each afternoon she tackled more of the boxes from the attic then showered and cooked dinner. One night she'd tried lasagna, based on the success of the spaghetti, and another evening had cooked some veggie chili with three kinds of beans. That hadn't gone over as well. Troy had made some comment about Yankees not knowing real Texas chili. Hers, he proclaimed, was pretty good bean stew.

She didn't want to take it personally, but she was still disappointed in him. He'd tried to put her off by giving the calves outrageous names. Well, he'd done just the opposite. He'd made her more determined than ever to save them.

On Thursday, Raven went to Graham to upload and print more photos and mail them to Mrs. Philpot, then drove back to the café in Brody's Crossing for lunch with her friends. Ida Bell volunteered to "foster" the rose cuttings when Raven left town, and offered to call another one of her friends from nearby Olney to come out and possibly identify the herbs.

They also talked about food, since Raven had found only a handful of yellowed, faded index cards in the back of a drawer at the Crawford ranch. They featured recipes for cakes and cookies, so they didn't help her with savory ingredients. After talking to the ladies about the way their grandmothers had cooked, Raven had a better idea what types of dishes might have been prepared on a turn-of-the-century Texas ranch, so she could guess which herbs they'd grown there. Heritage garden restoration wasn't an exact science, she reminded herself whenever she got frustrated at the lack of documentation.

"Raven, you should get your ends trimmed," Clarissa advised as they finished lunch. "Come by the salon after we pay the check and I'll take care of that for you."

Raven looked at her hair. She never thought about it much. It just…was. Thick and curly, she wore it long because that was easy. She could tie it back or clip it up. She didn't have to style it, and she wasn't good at that, anyway.

Her mother had always said her hair was a mess, that she couldn't do a thing with it when Raven was little. Raven had resented that attitude, until she had to do her own hair. She suspected her hair must be like her biological father's, and that was why her mother disliked it so. Her mother's hair was sleek, straight and light brown, now tinged with gray.

"Okay, I suppose I can come by."

An hour and a half later, she left the salon with a lot less hair. Clarissa had cut off about three inches after she'd washed and conditioned it, plus she'd given Raven a facial and waxed her eyebrows. She still wasn't sure how the hairdresser had talked her into it. Until this afternoon, she hadn't been aware that she needed such "improvements." No one, including her friend, Della, or her knitting-guild members, had ever suggested she have a makeover.

Clarissa wouldn't even let her pay. She said that the mineral supplements Raven had suggested for leg cramps had been worth more than a few snips and some "zip-zip" waxing. Raven knew better, but she didn't argue. Besides not having a lot of extra money, she didn't want to fall out with her new friend.

She arrived back at the ranch in time to make dinner, but after looking for Troy in the office and barn, she found a note taped to her bedroom door. "I'm going to Dewey's for a while," she read aloud. "Don't wait on me for dinner. I'll eat something there."

She looked down at Riley. "Something like a big steak," she told the dog. Riley seemed to grin. He was no doubt looking forward to another steak bone. Raven had found the other one gnawed down and buried beneath some hay in the barn. Riley wasn't good at hiding his transgressions. Or Troy's, for that matter.

"Okay, it's you and me," she told Riley, and headed into the kitchen to fix a big salad and some goat cheese toasted bread. It seemed Troy just couldn't help falling back into his old eating habits every so often.

Then, it suddenly occurred to her, did he have a date? Was he taking another woman to eat at Dewey's? And which possible scenario did she care about more?

LATE THAT NIGHT, RILEY WOKE Raven with a few light "wuffs." He jumped down from the bed. Raven didn't hear anything, but thought she'd better go investigate. She wasn't sure what time it was or even if Troy was home.

She grabbed her cotton robe and pulled it on over her sleep shirt. "Be quiet," she advised Riley, who stood at the door. He didn't seem alarmed, just curious. When she opened the door, he bolted into the hallway. Raven followed when she saw low light coming from the open doorway of the office.

She watched Troy for a moment. He sat behind the desk. The computer monitor was on and illuminated his face with a blue-green glow. He held a framed photo in one hand and absently scratched Riley's ears with the other.

"Hi," she said softly.

"Hi, yourself." He put the photo down and looked up. His face appeared drawn. Tired. Maybe something else. "You look…different."

"Clarissa trimmed my hair and…did some other stuff."

"You look nice."

"I probably look sleepy. Messy."

"Not really."

She fiddled self-consciously with her newly trimmed ends. "Did you have a good time at Dewey's?"

"It was okay. Not as much fun as last Saturday night," he said with a slight smile.

"Do any dancing?"

"No. I didn't have anyone to dance with."

Raven folded her arms and held in her joy. "Oh, I'll bet you could have found someone."

"Yeah, I guess so, but then both Caroline Brody and Venetia Taylor would be fighting over me, and who wants that kind of hassle?"

Her stomach suddenly felt empty. "Venetia and Caroline?"

"Both around sixty."

"Oh." Raven looked down at her bare feet, relieved and resenting it. "Were you working on the computer tonight?"

"Just checking a few things on the extremely slow Internet. I think I'm going to have to get a satellite card for my laptop."

"That would be nice. For you, I mean."

"You can use it, too."

"Thanks." She looked down again. She'd probably be gone before there was a faster Internet connection here.

"I'm sorry I woke you."

"You didn't. I suppose Riley heard or sensed you. You might have noticed that he loves you."

"Some dogs like men more than women. Some like women better. I think Riley adores you, too."

"Maybe, but he thinks you're the 'big dog.'"

"That's me." He took another look at the photo before turning off the computer and getting up from his chair. "I guess it's time to turn in."

Raven stepped around the other side of the desk and nudged the photo. "This is you, your brother and your mother?"

"A long time ago."

"Has she been gone long?"

"Right after that photo was taken."

"She looks so pretty. She doesn't look sick. It must have been sudden."

"Sudden? If you call packing your bags and walking out of the house while your kids are in school 'sudden,' then yes, it was."

"She left you? I thought…when you said 'gone' I though she was dead."

"She is now, but not then. She just left one day when I was fourteen and Cal had just turned eighteen."

"Oh, Troy."

He took the photo and put it in a drawer. "It's okay. It was a long time ago." He reached for the desk lamp and turned it off. Only the stove light from the kitchen illuminated the house, leaving the office in the dark. "Like I said, time to turn in."

She walked toward the doorway. He did the same. She stopped to let him pass, and so did he. They stood there for a moment at an impasse, when she decided she needed to say something else.

"I understand about having issues with your mother. I do, too, although mine didn't leave me." She reached out and patted his shoulder. "I'm really very sorry."

"I don't want your pity," he said just above a whisper, his tone fierce. She had only a moment to register alarm before he reached out and grasped her upper arms. "Don't treat me like one of your damn wounded animals," he growled as his head descended.

His lips locked over her mouth before she could make a sound. Fierce and strong, his hands pulled her to him as he angled his head. He tasted of beer and smelled a little of cigarette smoke, but she didn't care. Her lips parted and the kiss turned wild.

She couldn't keep herself from responding, from kissing him back as if she'd never stop. As if she didn't want him to stop. Ever. Her fingers grasped his shirt as she molded herself to him. Tight. And his hands held her there, against his hard body.

Suddenly she felt his hands on her arms again, felt him peeling her away from him. She opened her eyes to see and feel him breathing hard. He looked ragged, shocked. Like she felt.

What had just happened?

"I shouldn't have done that," he said in a low, hoarse voice. "I shouldn't have kissed you."

"No—"

"Go to bed, Raven. Alone." He turned and hurried out

of the room as if she was going to run him down and make him stay. She wouldn't do that. Would she? Two minutes ago she would have sworn she'd never kiss Troy Crawford as if her very life depended on it.

Chapter Eleven

The next morning before dawn, Troy regretted going to Dewey's last night almost as much as he regretted kissing Raven. He hadn't been drunk last night, but he was feeling those beers he'd had at the bar and later, sitting in the office, alone, where he'd gotten all moody about things. Things he could usually sweep under the rug. And then Raven had walked in, all sleep-warm and smelling of flowers and woman.

He shouldn't have kissed her, but he couldn't have stopped himself once she got that I-pity-you expression on her face and touched him. She'd made him angry and still he wanted her, against all common sense.

He rolled out of bed and went into the bathroom. After washing up, he downed three extra-strength pain relievers with a large glass of water. He was sore from working with those crazy cows. He'd forgotten how much he hated this time of year. Vaccinations, castrations, tagging. You definitely used a different set of muscles than you did at the gym.

He splashed water on his face again and combed his hair, which was standing up like a Mohawk. Today was Friday, right? They'd be finished with the hardest work by tonight and he could relax a little over the weekend. Just a little, though, because around a ranch, the chores were never done.

Right now, he'd just about sell this ranch for a dollar, jump in his comfortable SUV and drive back to his condo as if the hounds of hell were chasing him.

He dressed and walked into the kitchen. No coffee. No Raven. Just as well. He needed some time before he saw her. He heard Riley scratching at Raven's door, hurried back down the hallway and opened it. The dog bounded out but the room beyond him remained dark and quiet.

"Come on, boy," he whispered to the dog. "Let's go to the barn." He needed to get the horses ready for another long day. On the way out, he handed a grateful Riley the T-bone he'd saved from Dewey's last night.

Slowly, the morning sky lightened to pinks and purples. With all the horses fed and the tack out ready to saddle, he had time for coffee and a fried-egg sandwich before the hands arrived.

RAVEN EASED HER WAY INTO the kitchen, unsure of how she would react to Troy this morning. She was astonished that he'd kissed her, amazed and angry at her reaction. She would not have imagined that a kiss could be so... powerful. Kisses, in her experience, were occasionally fun, mostly pleasant and sometimes exciting. But Troy's kiss—their kiss—had been arousing, breath-stopping and life-changing.

She hadn't been ready. He'd surprised her. She'd been nice and friendly, and he'd laid an ambush.

But what now? She stopped at the open doorway. He wasn't here. Neither was Riley. They must still be in the barn. Raven had an urge to quickly make coffee and retreat to her room. She wasn't ready to see Troy yet.

She may never be ready to see him again.

She quickly filled the aluminum percolator with cold water, then measured grounds into the basket. Just as she was putting it into the base, the back door burst open and Riley ran in. Troy stepped into the kitchen, a stunned look on his face, and the basket of coffee grounds fell from her fingers. It plunked and rolled under the table as she watched Troy shut the door and stare at her as if he wondered what she was doing.

"I was making coffee for you," she answered the imagined question.

"You didn't have to," he said as he walked toward the table.

Raven grabbed the dustpan and broom and knelt on the floor. Coffee grounds were everywhere. She started sweeping them up. Suddenly, Troy hunkered down in front of her and handed her the empty basket. "I'm sorry I made you drop the coffee."

"It was my fault. I wasn't expecting you, but I shouldn't have overreacted." She took a deep breath and kept brushing. "I wasn't sure how I'd feel this morning, seeing you."

"I'm sorry I made you uncomfortable."

She nodded. "It was a mistake. I shouldn't have let it go on so long."

"You wish you hadn't endured my kiss?"

"I did more than endure it and you know it!" she said, looking up, angry that he was baiting her when she was barely holding on to her composure. "I participated, and I shouldn't have. I have no idea why, and I don't want to do that again."

"Fine. I was going to tell you it won't happen a second time."

"Good. We shouldn't… It's not a good idea."

"You're right. I told myself that, and anyway I kissed you last night, and I'm sorry."

"Okay then. Discussion over," she said, looking into his eyes.

"Yes, and we won't do it again," he confirmed.

"Right. Even more important."

"Right." He paused, then said, "We'll blame it on the beer…again."

"That's reasonable."

He stayed there for a moment too long. Enough time for her to see just a little bit of longing in his gaze. Enough to know that she probably looked the same way.

She scooted back as quickly as she could without spilling more coffee grounds. He jumped up, trying not to send the percolator basket flying.

"I'm going in there," he said, gesturing toward the hallway, the bath, his bedroom. Someplace where *she* wasn't.

"Okay. I'll see you later."

"Right," he said, retreating as fast as politely possible.

How would they get through the next week if they couldn't even clean up coffee grounds together?

TROY THOUGHT THE AFTERNOON would never end. He wished he could get the image of Raven, startled and unsure, out of his head, but he couldn't erase the memory of this morning, when he'd stepped into the kitchen. He really, really shouldn't have kissed her, not because it was morally wrong or even ill advised. No, he shouldn't have kissed her because now that's all he thought about, the feel of her lips melting to his, the tentative thrust of her tongue, the feel of her body pressed against him. He couldn't forget, and he couldn't do anything about it.

That seemed to be his fate lately. Ineffective frustration. First with his brother and the ranch, compounded by his family history, then capped off with Raven. What had he done to deserve this aggravation?

Like that guy Earl on the television show, maybe he needed to make a list and start working on his karma. Perhaps all that grief he'd given Raven over her food and beliefs was coming back to haunt him. Maybe someone up there was telling him to exercise better control, he thought at the end of the day as he entered the house. The quiet, empty house.

What could he do for Raven? He thought about what she valued. He couldn't do anything about the cattle, at least not yet. He had to make those decisions with his brother's best interests in mind. She loved her farm and her animals—heck, she loved *all* animals. She cared about the old homestead garden and the past.

That was it! He remembered his great-grandmother's spinning wheel in the attic, stuffed back under the eaves and forgotten for probably fifty years. He couldn't give Raven much, but he could present her with a piece of the past. His past. A link to the women who'd started and nourished the garden.

Before he took a shower or changed clothes, he went into the hallway and pulled down the stairs to the attic. With the boxes and trunk out of the way, it was easy to see the old spinning wheel, sitting there all alone. Yes, giving this to Raven was the right choice. No one in the Crawford family would ever use or appreciate it, while Raven would do both. At least, he supposed such an Earth Mother type as she would know how to spin. And even if the spinning wheel wasn't useful or didn't work, she would still like it for its style and history. She would see it as beautiful, while to him it was just an old, dusty attic ornament.

He took the spinning wheel to the barn. In the supply room he located linseed oil and old rags. He cleaned it as best he could. He'd have liked to sand it but she'd probably prefer the piece as authentic as possible. She liked old things, even if they weren't perfect.

Although he'd told her that she didn't talk about herself, he suddenly seemed to know a lot about her. How was that? Had their kiss magically infused him with knowledge? He didn't think so, but something strange was happening. Something he didn't have time to think about.

He carried the spinning wheel into the living room. He wished he had a bow or something to put on it, but that might be overkill. He'd casually show her after dinner.

Maybe he should take her out again. Maybe they could dance.

"You idiot," he told himself as he stripped out of his sweaty, dirty clothes in the bathroom. That type of thinking was exactly what they'd agreed they wouldn't do. No more kissing. No more situations that could lead to kissing. No more intimacy of any kind, including dark dance floors and beer drinking.

One more week. He had to control himself and be prudent for seven days. He could do that.

RAVEN WORKED ON THE GARDEN in the morning after feeding the calves and chickens, and collecting their eggs. When she came back to the house with plant samples, Ida Bell phoned.

"Can you come to town? We're having a meeting late this afternoon at the café."

"I'd be glad to," she replied, silently adding that she'd love to get away from the ranch, from Troy, if only for a little while. "What's the meeting about?"

"We have an idea to reopen the old farmers' market. I figured that you'd be a good person to talk to about that."

"I have a little experience, but it's all in New Hampshire."

"That doesn't matter. We need some good ideas. There are a few naysayers around here."

"I understand."

"We'll see you around four o'clock, then, at the café."

"I'll be there."

She looked down at Riley. "I have a date with my friends," she told the dog. "You and Troy are on your own for supper."

About three she showered and dressed. Her hair didn't behave as well as when Clarissa fixed it, so she decided to set off a little early and buy some new hair care products. If she was going to be vain, she might as well go all the way.

Raven left a note for Troy that she wouldn't be in for supper. Actually, the first time, she'd written "home" instead. She'd balled up that note and thrown it in the trash. When would she get the message that this ranch wasn't her home? She used the term from force of habit, she supposed. She'd lived in New Hampshire, in and around Manchester, all her life. This house wasn't even that homey.

After filling Riley's dish with soy dog chow, which she noticed he wasn't eating with any great enthusiasm, she grabbed a few of the plant specimens and her purse. If there were gardeners in town for the meeting, perhaps they could help her identify the plants that she thought might be herbs. The seedlings were so young, their leaves and stalks weren't fully developed and it was difficult to tell what they were.

She pulled in to the small parking lot next to Clarissa's House of Style. The café was only one block away, and the old farmers' market was almost adjacent to the beauty shop.

"Good afternoon, Clarissa," she said as she stepped inside the front door. A glass cabinet held nail-care products, while shelving against the wall displayed shampoos, conditioners, gels, mousse and sprays.

"Hi there, Raven," she said, looking up from the lady she was working on. "I'll be right with you. Have you met Caroline Brody? Her family was one of the original founders of Brody's Crossing. Caroline works part-time for her son, James. He's our one and only attorney in town."

"No, we haven't met. How are you?" She recalled the name from Troy's joke about Venetia Taylor and Caroline flirting with him at Dewey's.

Caroline Brody did not look like the kind of person who would be flirting with Troy. Not that Raven had taken him seriously. He liked to tease her. He didn't want to be taken at his word. He wanted to divert the truth. Fine. If he couldn't handle talking to her straight, she'd keep her distance. She needed to avoid him anyway.

"I'm just fine, thank you," the middle-aged lady said. She had graying blond hair and bright eyes. "I've heard a lot about you from Clarissa and Ida and a half dozen other people."

"Oh, really? I hope nothing bad."

"Oh, no. You're a real sensation around here. We don't get many vegetarians in cattle country. Of course, lots of people are concerned about additives and chemicals, so all that organic talk is popular right now."

"I hope it's more than talk," Raven said, not sure how to take Caroline's remarks.

"We're going to discuss it this afternoon, over at the café," Clarissa told Caroline as she whipped off the cape and brushed a few hairs off her neck. "All done."

After accepting payment and exchanging good-byes, Clarissa turned to Raven. "What can I do for you?"

"I'd like some new products like those you used on me the other day, but I want to make sure the manufacturers don't do any animal testing or add harmful chemicals."

"Let's take a look," Clarissa said. Raven was thankful the older lady didn't roll her eyes or advise Raven to stop being so sensitive.

They discovered the main supplier did not test on animals. The ingredients included many herbs, so Raven felt comfortable buying the shampoo, conditioner and styling gel.

"Any reason for this sudden interest in your hair?" Clarissa asked conspiratorially. She and Raven were the only people in the small salon.

"Not like you're thinking," Raven said. "Troy Crawford is the last person in the world I want to attract, inspire or otherwise influence."

"Really? What did that boy do?"

Raven shook her head. "I can't talk about it."

"Nothing bad, I hope. I mean, I heard he was at Dewey's last night and that he was moody, but I never thought he'd—"

"Oh, he didn't do anything…well, nothing harmful or illegal or anything like that."

Clarissa turned her head and gave Raven a sideways glance.

"Okay, he kissed me," Raven admitted. "We kissed." She shook her head. "It was a huge mistake. I think maybe he'd had a few beers. Not that it's a good excuse. I mean, *I* hadn't been drinking."

"So you kissed him back. That's not too bad, is it?"

"But we shouldn't have. We started out fighting, and then we decided to be nicer to each other so we could be friends. We didn't decide to *kiss*."

"Still, aren't you overreacting? He didn't put the heavy moves on you, did he?" Clarissa removed a dustpan and broom from the tall cabinet and started to sweep up Caroline Brody's blondish hair.

"No! We were talking about family—his family—and then he turned out the light because he was finished in the office, and then he pulled me to him and we kissed."

"Oh, his family. Well, that's a big mess."

"I know about his mother being…gone. He doesn't talk much about his father, except to say that he was stubborn. He said something once about his father not listening to his suggestions."

"That's a mild way to put it." Clarissa emptied the dustpan into the trash. "Troy looks more like his mother. He's sociable and his temperament is similar to hers, except he doesn't have the dark moods. He's more even-tempered. Luanna Crawford was probably a manic-depressive, but never diagnosed. She didn't fit with Calvin P. Crawford III."

"But Troy said his mother was interested in the old garden. That she worked with her mother-in-law to find out what was there and save the plants."

"Troy's grandmother didn't get along particularly well with her only son, but she did her duty to the ranch. She knew it was important to the family. She was a strong woman. A good woman. She liked Luanna but knew she wasn't all that stable. I knew them quite well because both

Crawford ladies got their hair done here, way back when I started the salon."

"I wish I'd known them," Raven said sincerely, with some wistfulness. Having no member of the past living on the ranch changed its dynamics. Troy was affected because he was alone. He knew that his plans for saving the ranch would be opposed by Cal. And yet, he was willing to do it anyway.

"I'm just pleased you're here to save that garden. There aren't many homesteads left."

"I know. I'm glad I found it, but it needs a lot of work."

"So," Clarissa said as she placed the dustpan and broom back in the tall cabinet behind her station, "you and Troy. That's not going anywhere?"

"No! Absolutely not. We've talked about it, agreed it was a mistake, and we're putting it behind us."

"Is he a good kisser?"

"Clarissa! You know I shouldn't answer personal questions."

Clarissa laughed. "So he is?"

Raven sighed. "Fantastic."

Clarissa smiled. "Let's get to that meeting."

AS RAVEN DROVE HOME FROM the first meeting of the Farmers' Market Rescue Committee, she felt very good about her stay in Brody's Crossing. She seemed to be a part of this community, for now. They'd even made her an honorary Texan. She'd reminded them that she was going back to New Hampshire soon, but they said it didn't matter. She would help them for as long as she was here. But they were friends she would keep for life.

Maybe one day, when she'd had some time to think about her stay here and Troy had moved back to Fort

Worth, she'd visit them. Perhaps by then the farmers' market would be a viable business. And she wouldn't cry when she saw cattle or wondered what had happened to the three calves.

She tried to shake off these sad thoughts as she entered the house through the back door. The kitchen smelled as if Troy had cooked supper for himself—something with beef and lots of spices. Riley was so glad to see her that she didn't have time to dwell on Troy's unhealthy choices. She knelt on the floor and rubbed the dog's furry coat, talking to him as he wagged his entire body.

She heard the television coming from the living room. Should she go to see Troy, or retreat to her bedroom? Or the office? No, she didn't want to face that room yet. If she went to say hi, it would appear that everything was back to normal. Yes, that would be best.

"Hello," she said as she walked toward the couch. Her knitting was right where she'd left it.

"Did you have a good meeting?" Troy asked, muting the television.

"Yes. We talked about reopening the farmers' market."

"That would be good, I suppose. Are there enough vendors around here, enough produce?"

"They believe so." She settled on the couch and picked up her knitting, Riley at her feet. Only then did she realize there was something new in the room.

"Where did you get that wonderful spinning wheel?"

"It was my great-grandmother's," he answered. "It's been in the attic for as long as I can remember. It was there when I was a child, and I saw it when I moved the boxes and trunk for you." He walked over to the gleaming old piece and spun the wheel. "It's for you."

She blinked, not sure she'd heard him. "What?"

"My brother and I have no interest in this type of thing. You appreciate the past, and you're restoring our great-grandmother's garden. I think she'd want you to have it." He paused, then frowned. "That is, if you want it."

"Oh, it's beautiful." She put her knitting down and walked toward the spinning wheel. "Are you sure?"

"Absolutely." He stepped back, as though he was afraid to get too close to her. "Besides, I wanted to tell you that I'm sorry. Again."

"Oh." She felt her face fall. "You don't have to keep apologizing."

"Maybe I don't feel as if I've done it right yet."

"We agreed that we were both at fault."

"Then why do I think you really blame me?"

Raven shrugged and spun the wheel. "Who knows? Maybe you're projecting."

"I don't think so."

"You're sorry. I'm sorry. Thank you for the spinning wheel," she said, breaking eye contact. "I'll take really good care of it."

"You're sure we're okay?"

"Yes, I'm sure. Please don't ask me again."

"Okay." He stood there for a moment, then asked, "Do you want to go to Dewey's tomorrow night for supper?"

She stood there, the spinning wheel between them, and longed to say yes. But that would be wrong. "No, I don't think that would be a good idea."

"You're probably right," he said, then turned away to his chair. In a moment, the television sound came back on. Raven settled back on the couch with her knitting.

Being strong was hard.

Chapter Twelve

Over the weekend Troy did a lot of research. He'd called friends, fellow ranchers and even people he'd never met. He debated whether to e-mail Cal. But what good would that do? Cal would be against anything Troy suggested, so maybe it was best to charge ahead with his plans. He needed to talk to the bank and see what they'd be willing to do if he presented them with a viable business strategy. The ranch's current level of indebtedness wasn't encouraging, but he wasn't giving up.

The ideas he was formulating weren't anything like the ones he would have suggested when he was younger. Back then, he'd wanted to raise rodeo stock and Brangus cattle. He'd wanted to grow their own hay, which actually still made sense. His proposals had been shot down before he'd been able to fully explain them. The Rocking C specialized in Herefords, his father had explained gruffly. Let someone else fool with producing and baling hay. And he didn't know squat about rodeo stock, and didn't want to learn.

Truer words had never been spoken. Cal had sat there and listened, not saying a thing. Later, when Troy asked him why he didn't at least suggest that their father consider his ideas, Cal had repeated what the old man had said. They raised Herefords. End of story.

Well, it was nearly the end of the story—the story of the Rocking C. But not quite. Now they were going to do something way different. He was glad there would be half a world between him and his brother when Cal got the news. As soon as Troy decided what the news would be, that is.

He stood up, his back a little stiff from sitting so long. The sun was still bright, but his stomach told him it was suppertime. He wandered into the kitchen and smelled something good simmering on the stove. Using a pot holder, he opened the lid and saw what looked like vegetable soup. Good, he liked soup, as long as she didn't put tofu or goat cheese in it.

"Raven?"

She must be outside. He slipped on his boots and strolled to the barn. Raven wasn't inside, but he could hear her. He walked out the barn door and around the side. She and Riley sat within the calves' pen, while Raven talked to them as if they were children.

Dammit. She'd gotten too close to those calves this past week. While he was busy culling the herd, she'd been making pets out of them. And it was his fault.

"Hey, Raven," he said.

She looked startled, but didn't jump up in case she spooked the calves. "Did you need me?"

Hell, yes, he needed her. Wanted her, too. "No, I just wondered what was up with supper. Is there anything I can do?"

"No, I've made vegetable-bean soup, and I'm baking corn bread. I thought I'd have it ready in about forty-five minutes."

"That's fine." He rested his hands on the fence. "You know this isn't a good idea, right?"

"I'm just killing time."

"They're cattle, not pets. I told you that."

"I know."

"I'm turning them out with the herd in a few days."

"No! They're still little."

"They're big enough. Besides, it's for the best. You'll be finishing up with the garden soon, and they need to get used to eating on their own."

She looked a bit distressed but didn't argue. *Thank God.* "I'll see you inside. Let me know if I can help with supper. You've been doing almost all of the cooking, and I appreciate it."

She nodded but didn't say anything. He went back to the house. He had a feeling supper was not going to be a real pleasant, talkative time at the Rocking C.

THE NEXT MORNING AFTER WORKING in the garden, Raven went to town to have lunch with Clarissa and the gang. Distress must have been evident on her face because Ida immediately asked, "What's wrong?"

Raven scooted into the bench seat. "Troy is turning the calves loose with the herd this week. They're going to be just more...more of his 'beef on the hoof.' I don't think I can stand it."

"Oh, hon, that's just reality here in cattle country," Clarissa said.

"But it's so cruel!"

Ida placed her hand over Raven's. "I'm sorry."

"Well, I just hate what Raven's going through," Bobbi Jean Maxwell said. "She's gotten used to those calves. Now he's taking them away."

Raven sniffed and rubbed her eyes. "Troy warned me not

to get attached. He told me all along that this is what he was going to do, but I never realized it would be so hard."

"Well, I don't see why it has to happen," Bobbi Jean said.

"What do you mean?" Ida asked.

"Raven's been taking care of those calves like they're her own. She loves them like pets. It's just not right to take them away from her now."

"But they are Troy's calves."

"He said they were Rocking C calves," Raven said, "but I never thought about what that would really mean."

"I know, hon," Clarissa said sympathetically.

"I'd gladly buy them if I could," Raven said. "I just don't have the money right now. I could send it after I get home, but I wouldn't have anyplace to keep them." She sniffed again. "They won't be calves forever."

"That's so true. They'll be big ol' beeves before long," Ida said.

Raven raked her hands through her hair. At least with her new cut and Clarissa's products, she could actually get her fingers through it. "I don't know what to do."

"Well, I think we should put those calves someplace safe," Bobbi Jean said.

"What do you mean?" Ida asked.

"We need to save them."

"How would we do that? I think Troy might notice if the calves disappeared," Raven said.

"Well, yes, but Raven could give him an IOU or work something out," Bobbi Jean suggested.

"I just don't see how you're going to back a cattle hauler or even a horse trailer up to the Crawford barn without him noticing," Ida said.

"Who said they needed to be moved in a cattle truck?"

Bobbi Jean threw the question out there, drawing everyone's attention.

"What do you have in mind?" Raven asked.

"Just that it wouldn't be odd if you asked a few of your friends to come out to the ranch to see your work on the garden, right?"

"Oh, Bobbi Jean, what are you planning?" Ida asked.

"Tell me more," Raven said.

TROY COULDN'T STAND THE COLD shoulder he was getting from Raven. She was polite, but gone were her smiles and the lectures on eating healthy meals. He didn't feel comfortable teasing her. He saw their rift caused her sadness also, and didn't want her last days here to be filled with the kind of estrangement and angst that he'd lived through for years in this house.

For the past two weeks, he'd experienced a new kind of friendship. He'd never shared his place with a woman before. Living with Raven wasn't like having a girlfriend, of course, because there wasn't anything sexual happening. Other than that kiss, he'd kept his hands to himself, even those times when Raven had impulsively touched him. He'd been proud of his self-control, because the more he got to know her, the better he liked her, even when she aggravated him.

Plus, whatever she'd had done at the beauty salon made her look even prettier. Her hair moved with more ease, and shined as if there were spotlights following her. Her face glowed and her eyes seemed brighter.

He'd try harder to mend fences with her. He didn't want her going back to New Hampshire until they were right with one another. So, when he came in late in the afternoon and saw her going through the produce in the refrigerator, he decided to take immediate action.

"If you don't have anything planned yet, I'd like to go out for dinner with you," he said.

She jumped, her eyes wide as she turned to face him. "Really, that's probably not a good idea."

"I think it is. We need to…talk." As much as he hated the implications of that word, he decided it might persuade her. And really, they did need to clear the air. How could they be friends if they didn't both decide to put their differences aside? That's what needed to happen.

"Talk?" He saw her swallow as she tentatively said the word that guys dreaded.

"Yeah, nothing serious." He shrugged. "I just miss chatting with you. And the last time we went out, we had fun. You know, like friends."

"Friends," she repeated.

"Yeah." He frowned. "If you're only replying in one-word answers, could you just say yes so I could take a shower? I'm really hungry."

She blinked, then seemed to relax. "Okay. Yes, we can go to dinner."

He let out a sigh, then nodded. "Good. I'll be ready in about a half an hour if that's okay." He didn't add that he was hungry enough to eat a side of beef.

AFTER DINNER THAT NIGHT, Raven excused herself to work in the office while Troy turned on the television. She wasn't sure if the hockey game was still on or if he was watching reruns, but as long as he was occupied for a short while, she was safe. She turned on the computer, then dialed Bobbi Jean Maxwell from the desk phone.

"Hi. Troy and I just got back from supper at Dewey's." Raven paused, then added, "Are we still on?"

"I'm ready whenever you are."

"Good. How about Thursday? Troy told me tonight that he's going to release the calves by the weekend."

"Oh, then Thursday sounds good. I'll call Ida."

"Okay. I'll tell Troy that the two of you are coming to see the garden."

"Sounds great."

"Are you sure?"

"I'm sure. We're friends. Friends help each other."

Raven felt tears gather but blinked them away. "Thank you."

"See you Thursday after lunch. Don't worry."

"I can't help it."

"If anything comes up to change our plans, let me know. But, in any case, we can still come out to see the garden."

"Thanks. Good night."

Raven hung up the phone and rested her forehead on her propped-up hands. Had she been a good enough actress to appear "normal" tonight at supper? She hoped so. Troy seemed to sense something was wrong, but he didn't have a clue what she'd planned. How could he? She could barely believe herself what she, Ida and Bobbi Jean were going to do.

After a moment, she went online and checked her e-mail. There was one from an herbal expert who suggested she resubmit photos of the seedlings she wanted identified in another week when they were bigger. There was one from Della giving her an update on the farm. She'd attached a couple of digital photos of Mr. Giggles and Ms. Pris on the couch. Her rabbit looked as if he was trying to steal a ball of yarn the cat was playing with. Raven smiled, missing them all.

"Cute picture."

She jumped. "You snuck up on me."

"I didn't sneak. I guess you were just busy looking at the photo."

"They are cute. I miss them."

"I know." Troy reached down and kneaded her shoulders. "You're way too tense."

"Ouch!" He'd found the muscles that always tightened from her shoulder to her neck. She wiggled in the desk chair to get away from the pressure. "I guess I am. You need to be gentle."

Troy's hands paused a moment, then began to rub more slowly. Lighter. "I can be gentle," he said softly.

Suddenly she felt him bend closer to her and saw the shadow of him in the computer monitor, superimposed over the photo of her pets. What a bizarre combo. She closed her eyes and tried very hard to resist the whisper of his breath, then the sensation of his lips, on her neck.

"That's not a massage," she whispered.

"I'm doing it with my lips. Gently," he replied, his voice low and oh, so sexy.

"I thought we weren't going to do this type of thing."

"What type of thing?"

"Kissing and...stuff."

"I'm not kissing you. I'm helping you relax."

Relax? She was wound so tight she felt as if she might fly apart at any minute. On the other hand, she wanted to melt into his hands and lips and whatever else he pressed against her.

"You're a dangerous man," she said quietly.

"You're a provocative woman."

"I haven't been provoking you," she protested, feeling a surge of outrage. She'd been careful...especially since she was hiding such a big secret about the calves.

"Darlin', you just being here provokes me. It makes me want to do all kinds of rash things. Like throw you over my shoulder, take you to my bed and slam the door shut for a good long time. Your presence makes me want to grab that pretty, shiny hair, hold on tight, and kiss you senseless, until you stop arguing with me and let me do all that 'stuff' I'm thinking about."

"Um, what stuff?" she asked, rolling her head and neck against his cheek, his lips. Her eyes popped open when what he'd really suggested sank into her muddled brain. "I mean, what are you talking about? That sounds so chauvinistic. Kind of violent. And maybe painful."

He chuckled, looking at her in the now screen-saver-enabled monitor. Tiny stars raced past his image. The effect made her dizzy. His warm breath made her crazy.

"Trust me, darlin', I would never do anything to hurt you...unless you asked me real nice."

"Troy?"

"Yes?"

"Please—"

"I thought you'd never ask," he murmured before he reached down and lifted her right out of the desk chair.

Her arms clung to his neck out of self-preservation. He held her high against his chest and lowered his head to kiss her neck again. Shivers danced through her body.

"I'm too heavy."

"You don't weigh hardly any more than a newborn calf."

Calf. Calves. She closed her eyes and groaned, which

he no doubt mistook for desire. Well, she was feeling that for sure. Wild, tingly, crazy desire for someone she shouldn't be doing this with.

"Hang on," he whispered. He started walking, turning her through the office doorway, striding down the hall as she hung on tight.

"We shouldn't—" she tried to say.

"Yes, we should. Don't you believe in fate? What are the odds that you'd end up here, on a cattle ranch? Or that I would be absolutely crazy to make love to you, when you aggravate me so much?"

He laid her gently on the bed. His bed. She raised up and looked around. She'd never been in his room before. She hadn't dared, afraid to intrude, to get too personal. As long as she didn't picture him here, naked or nearly so, she could sleep just down the hallway.

"I thought you'd have a king-size bed with mirrors on the ceiling," she said.

"Naw, that's at my condo in Fort Worth," he said with a grin, "along with the handcuffs and feathers."

"Feathers?"

"Never mind. Now, where was I?" He lowered his body slowly, settling his legs inside her thighs, holding himself up with his forearms. He pressed against her where she hadn't been pressed against in a long, long time.

He dropped his head and nuzzled her neck, his chest barely teasing her breasts. In seconds, she was straining against him, rubbing, holding him close. Still, he didn't kiss her. She wanted to scream.

"Kiss me," she demanded, nearly panting.

"We agreed no more kisses," he said, which made no

sense because he was kissing her everywhere except her lips. Well, not everywhere, but a girl could dream.

"I think, considering we're lying on your bed, that you can kiss me now."

"That's good, because I was going to in about ten seconds whether you said it was okay or not." And then he stopped talking and started kissing, and all logical arguments flew out of her head. This was better than before, maybe because she didn't have to concentrate on standing up. All she needed to do was lie there and feel his firm lips on hers, his hot, searching tongue and his even hotter hands.

She kissed him back with all the passion inside her, all the longing she'd held in check for the past two weeks. They seemed to battle for air and dominance as they rolled over on the bed. She held his face in her hands, then wound her arms around his neck, while he began exploring her body. *Yes,* she wanted to tell him, but she wasn't sure she spoke the word aloud. Her blood was pounding too loud in her ears. Her heart felt as if it might burst.

They struggled with clothes. She pulled his shirt from his jeans; he raised her skirt to her thighs and explored the smooth edge of her panties. She rolled him over again, searching for his belt buckle. Her skirt flowed around them, and she knew it had to come off. Now. How else would she be able to see all of him once she got those jeans unbuttoned?

"How do you undo this thing?" he asked, as if he read her mind.

"It's tied in front." She sat up on him with her thighs on either side of his hips, and reveled in the feel of his hardness pressed against her. *Yes, right there,* she felt like saying. She found the bow and slipped it free. She bunched the skirt in her fist and raised it over her head, letting it sail across the room and land somewhere in the darkness.

"Nice technique," he said, reaching up for her gauzy blouse. He unbuttoned her with amazing speed, and she shrugged out of it. She sat on him dressed only in her thin camisole and panties.

"You're overdressed," she said, running her hands down the front of his shirt. She grabbed the loose ends and peeled it apart, popping the pearly snaps one by one, until his hard abs and wide chest were revealed. "I wish I could see you better," she whispered.

"No problem," he said, swiveling his upper body to reach for the bedside lamp. The motion pressed him even harder to her and she gasped. "I want to see you, too," Troy said. "All of you."

Again they struggled, to remove his shirt, to shed his jeans. He finally gave up and rolled off her. He pushed out of his socks and Levi's, and stripped his plain white boxers down his legs as he turned back to her. *No, wait,* she wanted to say. *Let me look.* But he reached for her and she let him take the camisole and pull it off.

"Nice," he whispered with some reverence. "Very nice."

"I'm not that well endowed," she said, hoping he was sincere. She'd expected a cowboy to prefer bigger breasts. Someone who'd fill out one of those western shirts and threaten to pop a few snaps.

"You're perfect. You look just like I'd imagined you."

"When did you imagine me?"

"When didn't I? Just every night, all night, and every morning. And most of the time during the day."

No man had ever said anything like that to her. She'd always thought she wanted poetic endearments, but having someone admit that he constantly thought about her naked was way more arousing.

"I've thought about you, too," she admitted. "But not too much or I wouldn't have gotten anything done." She ran her hand over his chest, down his side, around his abs where the line of hair leading from his chest beckoned her lower. "You look better, you feel better, than anything I could have imagined."

"I'm going to make you feel even better," he promised, and rolled her over onto her back. Kneeling, he stripped off her panties and threw them in the direction of her skirt. Then he looked, and then he touched. Not tentatively, but he molded her. Shaped her beneath him as he lowered himself once more.

Their kisses turned hotter. His hands stayed greedy. She couldn't get enough of his lean, muscled body, just as he needed to devour her. This was insanity, but she willingly participated. She could not have stopped herself if her life depended on it.

When she could stand no more, when he could barely breathe, he opened the nightstand drawer and grabbed a handful of condoms. They landed around their steaming bodies, sticking to their damp skin. He found one, ripped it open and sheathed himself.

Their movements merged into a blur of heat and passion and yearning. Raven held him tight and he gave all of himself. She never wanted the night to end, yet she searched for release with greedy abandon. And finally, when he whispered in her ear, "Come fly with me, Raven," she let go and joined him in explosions that surely lit the room, the ranch, the state, in a white-hot blaze.

Chapter Thirteen

During the early-morning hours, as Troy slept in naked splendor with a smile on his face and the sheet bunched in his fist, Raven slipped out of his bedroom. She didn't dare grab her clothes, which were all over the place. She'd get them tomorrow while Troy was working. She'd find her things when he wasn't around, because she wasn't sure she could face him again so soon.

She wanted to ask herself, *What were you thinking?* However, she already knew the answer; she was thinking that this felt so good. Way too good to stop. She knew she and Troy shouldn't make love, and yet they had. Now what? Now she had to face the consequences that she'd pushed aside when she'd felt, well, way too good to stop. And think.

Very quietly, she ran water over her hands and splashed her face. She wasn't an uptight person. She wasn't a prude, she thought as she rubbed her eyes. But last night's…encounter went way beyond what she could have imagined. She never would have thought she'd react to Troy as she did. They'd felt so right together, but that didn't mean they were meant for each other. As a matter of fact, they weren't destined to have any sort of relationship. Except for a mistake over an old database, brought about by a twenty-something-year-old letter, they would never have met, she reminded herself as she stared in the mirror.

In less than a week, they would part. As much as she'd enjoyed making love with Troy, she had to prepare for that moment. She would walk out the door to her car, and she'd never see him again. And that was that.

Oh, she knew it wasn't what she wanted. She had allowed herself to feel too much, as if she could have stopped her passion and Troy's desire from colliding. She could have tried harder, though. Leaving would be so painful that she wondered how she'd endure the moment when she drove away.

She wouldn't call this love. She wouldn't give a name to her feelings. But oh, she wanted to acknowledge what was in her heart. Just once. Just to hear those words…

A tiny whimper escaped her. She thought she might cry, but she did her best not to. She'd never known a man like Troy Crawford, and deep down inside, where her instincts and special feelings resided, she knew she never would again. He was a one-of-a-kind occurrence in her life, while she would be just that silly Yankee vegetarian farmer who happened to stay at the ranch one May.

Tonight shouldn't have happened. She wasn't going to get over Troy for a long, long time, if ever, and he would forget about her before the summer wildflowers faded and died.

TROY WOKE BEFORE DAWN WITH the strangest sense of peace, as if suddenly all the planets had lined up. The night came back to him and he remembered everything. Raven. She was the reason he felt so good this morning. Now, if he'd woken up with her in his arms, it would have been the perfect start to the day.

He frowned. Where was she? When had she left him? He'd been sound asleep, that was for sure, if he'd missed her going. He needed to talk to her, to find out why she hadn't stayed in his bed.

If they only had a few days, maybe a week, together, he wanted to spend as much time as possible with Raven. She was a heck of a lot more woman than he'd imagined when she'd first arrived at the ranch.

Troy smiled to himself as he walked naked to the door. He looked into the hallway, but it was empty and dark. Her bathroom was quiet, as well, and Raven's door appeared to be closed. Who would have thought that he'd be so infatuated with an argumentative Yankee vegetarian? No one he knew. As a matter of fact, if anyone had considered the possibility, they would have bet against it. Yet here he was, wanting her again. Still. For as long as she was in Brody's Crossing.

He couldn't bear to think about her leaving, although he knew she must. She had a life to go back to. He had a ranch to save. The two were mutually exclusive, and yet...he would have enjoyed spending more time with her.

He thought of going into her room, waking her, making love to her one more time before morning chores. But she probably needed her sleep, and he needed to work. He had a good idea that he'd get a lot accomplished today and would be ready to turn in real early tonight. With Raven.

RAVEN WAITED UNTIL TROY left the kitchen for the barn before she rolled out of bed. She felt sore in unaccustomed places, and her heart was bruised, as well. Still, she had to talk to Troy sooner or later. No telling what he was thinking this morning. He could either assume they'd go at it like bunnies for as long as she was here, or he might look on last night as a nice interlude that he didn't want to repeat, or he could get all serious and want to talk again.

She had to do the talking. She needed to tell him that while she'd enjoyed making love and would treasure the memories, it wasn't a good idea to continue.

Yes, as soon as he returned.

She pulled on her robe, washed her face and brushed her teeth, and then made coffee for him. While she waited, she brewed herself some English Breakfast tea and fixed scrambled eggs. She put goat cheese in hers and commercially-grated cheddar in his. Wasn't that just a perfect example of their differences? They couldn't even eat the same breakfast. About the time she thought he'd walk through the door, she toasted some dark bread under the broiler and waited.

He came in with a smile on his face and the smells of the outdoors on his clothing. Behind him, the window reflected the pink and orange and purple of the sunrise. She tried her best to seem pleasant and happy. Or, at least, not unhappy.

"Hi there, sunshine," he said, coming over to the table and kissing her forehead as she shielded her lips with her tea mug. "I'm going to wash up, then I'll be back for breakfast. It smells almost as good as you."

As soon as he walked out of the room, she put her mug down and covered her eyes with her hands. *Please, give me strength to get through this,* she prayed to anyone— God, Mother Earth or a stray Greek deity—who might be listening.

She placed the food on the table and watched him stride

back into the kitchen, all bubbly energy this morning. So, he was one of those people. She'd never seen him quite like this. At any other time, she'd be pleased that she'd caused him to feel good, to have more drive. Today, it was as if she were about to kick a puppy.

"I made yours with cheddar," she said softly.

"That was real sweet of you," he replied with a smile, digging in to his eggs, using his strong white teeth—the very teeth that had nibbled their way down her body last night—to tear into the thick bread.

She waited until he'd finished. She played with her eggs, eating some, pushing the rest under her piece of toast. Then, when he took his plate to the sink and washed it off, she turned and said, "Last night was great."

"Yes, it was." He came over and hunkered down in front of her chair, so their eyes were nearly level. He fingered one strand of her hair. "Who would have thought that we'd share that kind of chemistry? You coming to this ranch was the very nicest surprise." And then he leaned forward and kissed her. She tried very hard not to respond.

When he pulled back and frowned a little, she said, "It was lovely, but since I'm leaving soon, I don't think we should do it again."

"What?"

"Like you said, we're very different people. Yes, we created some sparks, but that isn't always a good thing."

"It felt really good to me, and I think to you, too."

"Many things do that are bad for us."

"What we did wasn't illegal, immoral or fattening. Why not take advantage of that chemistry? I don't understand your reasoning."

"I've spent most of my life denying myself things that

look harmless on the outside yet are very damaging. Do you have any idea how difficult it is for me to avoid wearing leather shoes, belts or purses? And not eating meat. That's hard at times, but I believe it's wrong, for me and for the animals. I can't change that, Troy. Please don't ask me to."

"I'm not trying to change your beliefs, Raven. I'm trying to understand why we can't enjoy ourselves like consenting adults. This isn't like being a vegetarian."

"It's exactly like that," she said, rising from the chair to put space between herself and Troy. "I care for you. Maybe too much, and I'm going to leave. Soon. The more time I spend with you…intimately, the harder it is to go. I'd love to spend every night with you, but it's not good for me. For us."

"You don't know that," he said, but his voice lacked conviction.

"Yes, I do. And I think you do, too."

"I'll tell you what I know. I want to be with you. I want to make love with you. Every chance I get."

Raven shook her head. "I can't, Troy. Please don't ask me to go against what I know is right for me."

She nearly ran out of the kitchen, back to the relative safety of her bedroom. No, not her room. The guest bedroom. She was a guest at this ranch, and her time was running out.

She sat on the bed and listened to sounds from the kitchen. Running water again. The scrape of a chair moved across the floor, shoved against the table. Then, finally, the slam of the back door. He was gone, and at last, she let the tears flow.

BY THURSDAY MORNING, TROY had come to some decisions regarding the ranch. He still wasn't sure it could be viable. He resented Cal's attitude, and if their father were alive, he'd argue with him man to man about his stubborn insistence that he was always right.

He entered the kitchen for lunch that day, but didn't see Raven in the house. As usual. They'd resorted to communicating through notes. He'd reminded her that the calves had to be turned out with the herd. She'd told him that she'd be using the computer later that night. Maybe in a couple of days, he could talk to her again, but for now, he couldn't say the things he would like her to know.

He wanted to grab her, kiss her, make her understand that they should be together. She had to be ready to listen, though, and she wasn't. He wouldn't give up hope. A passion that explosive shouldn't be denied forever. If only once more before she left, he had to have her. He wanted the closure that making love would bring.

He dragged his hand through his hair and groaned. He couldn't believe he'd just thought about "closure." How wussy was that? It only showed how tied in knots Raven had him. It proved they really needed to have sex one more time. Before they did the deed, though, they'd each agree that it was physical, that they were friends, and that they were adults. There would be no hurt feelings then.

Raven had left him a note this morning that a few of her friends—his neighbors—were coming over to see the garden after lunch. He wrote a note back that he had a meeting with the banker at two o'clock. Apparently they wouldn't be seeing each other much today. With a sigh, he headed for the shower.

"THIS IS PERFECT TIMING," RAVEN said as Bobbi Jean backed her van up to the barn.

"It's fate," the older lady said, looking in the rearview mirror. Ida stood near the barn door, giving her friend backing-up directions. "He's gone and you can claim you turned the calves out with the herd."

"I'm not sure I'll be very good at lying," Raven said.

Bobbi Jean had volunteered her fully-loaded van to transport the calves. She'd taken out all the movable items and placed plastic sheeting, the kind used for painting projects, on the carpet "just in case." Raven thought that was a good idea.

Ida had contributed a ramp that had been used by her mother-in-law after she was confined to a wheelchair. With luck, the calves would go up the ramp, into the van, and be driven to Ida's friend's ranch in Olney. After that, Raven would make arrangements for their permanent home. It was a simple plan, which was always the best kind.

The only thing Raven had to do was come up with the money to reimburse Troy for the loss of the calves. She didn't know how much that would be, but she'd leave a check for him. Or a deposit and an IOU if they were more expensive than she thought.

With a sigh, she opened the passenger door. "I guess it's time."

Ida walked around to the driver's side as Bobbi Jean got out. "I never thought I'd be rustling calves."

"We're not rustling. We're moving stock that Raven is buying on credit."

"Excellent way to look at it," Ida said.

"I just hope Troy understands when he finds out," Raven said.

"Oh, that will be days from now. He'll calm down."

I sure hope so, Raven added silently.

"GRAB THE ROPE!" IDA SHOUTED to Raven as the van traveled as slowly as traffic allowed toward Highway 114.

"I can't control them all," Raven said. She held one calf against her and was trying to press another up against the cabinets in the back of the van. The animals had gotten more distressed as the vehicle carried them farther from the ranch. A short time ago, one of the calves had almost forced its way through the bucket seats into the front. Now Raven and Ida had their hands full while Bobbi Jean drove.

Suddenly, the calves started with the vocal objections. They seemed to be braying like donkeys. The sounds agitated them even more, and they banged against the van's fittings as Raven and Ida tried to keep them contained.

"Maybe this isn't a good idea," Raven said.

"Do you want me to turn around?" Bobbi Jean asked.

"Are we near Olney?" Raven asked.

"No, not really. We're still getting out of Brody's Crossing, maybe a fourth of the way."

"I don't know! If we go back, what will we do with them? I don't have another option."

"I could go fetch my horse trailer," Ida volunteered.

"Troy would surely see it," Raven said.

"Watch out!" Ida shouted as one of the calves broke free. It immediately headed for the wide-open spaces of the windshield.

A second calf squirmed loose from Raven. "Aargh!" She lunged for its hind legs. The ungrateful beast kicked her, then it, too, headed for the front. "Bobbi Jean, watch out!"

The van swerved as the calf's rear bumped against the steering wheel. The animal landed in the front seat, sitting there as if it were a dog.

"I have to pull over."

"Okay. I'll try to get the calves under control."

"No, I mean, there's a police car behind us with its lights on."

"Oh, no!"

"Oh, yes," Bobbi Jean replied.

Raven buried her head in the last calf, the one that was always better tempered than the other two mischief-makers, and felt like crying. "This is not happening."

"Just be calm. Tell the police officer that you bought the calves."

The cop came to the window, not even looking inside the van. Okay, maybe they'd be okay. "License and registration, please," he asked Bobbi Jean.

As she reached for her purse, the calf in the front seat let out a loud and plaintive cry. Raven watched in horror as the officer looked across the van, pulled his sunglasses off and looked again.

"Is that a calf?"

"Why, yes, it is," Bobbi Jean answered easily. "He's a pet."

The other two calves, not to be outdone, chose that moment to try and join their friend. They started jumping around, stomping on Raven's foot and making her cry out in pain. The officer looked into the back.

"I suppose these are his buddies, right?"

"Yes, you could say that."

He glared at Bobbi Jean. "Don't even try to tell me you're taking them to Six Flags for a playdate."

Chapter Fourteen

"She's accused of *what?*" Troy almost shouted into his cell phone as he stood in the middle of the bank lobby.

Lots of heads turned as the police chief, Leonard Montoya, answered, "Rustling."

"What are you talking about?" He grabbed his paperwork, gestured what he hoped would be considered "later" to the banker and stalked outside.

"Three calves were found in a van owned by Bobbi Jean Maxwell. Raven York claimed responsibility."

"I'm next door. I'll be right there."

He flipped the phone closed. Dammit. Rustling? It didn't take a genius to figure out whose calves they were.

He was in the police station within thirty seconds. "I'm looking for Raven York. She's being held on suspicion of cattle rustling."

"Oh, yeah. She's with Chief Montoya and Officer Jackson in the conference room, down the hall, first door on the right. That's the only space we have that will hold everyone. You're Troy Crawford, aren't you?"

"That's right. I assume it's my calves she's accused of stealing."

"Probably. I'll buzz you back."

"Thanks." Troy stood at the door and waited to hear the locks disengage, then strode into the room. Raven sat between the chief and the officer, her hands folded in her lap. Or was she handcuffed? The idea of her being arrested and detained was bad enough, but for her to be cuffed was too much.

"Raven, are you okay?"

She nodded.

"Can I see your hands?"

She looked at him with big dark eyes, slow to respond, and finally lifted her arms to the table. He felt himself relax. She wasn't restrained.

"Mr. Crawford, I'm Chief Montoya. I know your brother, but we haven't met."

"No. Can you tell me what happened?"

"Ms. York and her friends, Ida Bell and Bobbi Jean Maxwell, were arrested on State Highway 16 in Ms. Maxwell's van. They were in possession of three calves that Ms. York says belong to you."

"I knew you were going to get too attached to those animals," he said.

"So you confirm that they're your calves Ms. York stole?" Chief Montoya asked.

"I didn't say that."

"I didn't think I was stealing them," Raven said in a small voice. Troy felt his insides churn. Raven wasn't the kind of woman who spoke in a small voice. She should be lecturing them now about the evils of eating beef.

"That's right. She was going to pay for them," Ida said.

"Raven didn't do anything wrong," Bobbi Jean added.

"Facts are facts," the officer said.

"Where were the calves?" Troy asked.

"Well, one of them was in the front seat of a fully-loaded 1987 teal-blue van driven by Mrs. Maxwell. The other two were in the back with Ms. York and Mrs. Bell," Officer Jackson explained.

"The front seat?" Troy asked. "How did a calf get in the *front* seat of a van?"

"The point here, Mr. Crawford, is that the calves were being transported from your ranch to an undisclosed ranch in Olney."

"Raven?" he asked.

"I wrote you a note," she said.

Troy ran a hand through his hair. "Could I talk to Raven alone?"

"Well, considering she's not a violent criminal, I suppose that's okay. I'll give you five minutes, then I want to get this settled. We do have other business."

"Thanks, Chief." He'd bet his SUV that the Brody's Crossing Police Department didn't have anything more interesting or pressing to do today, but if the chief wanted to pretend he was on a deadline, that was fine.

"Come on, ladies. I'll get you a cup of coffee," the chief told Ida and Bobbi Jean.

Raven stared at her hands in the silence of the nearly empty conference room. Troy waited for her to speak, and when she didn't, he took a seat across from her. He didn't trust himself to sit next to her. His emotions were too jumbled. "Tell me what happened."

She took a deep breath. "You were right about the calves. Once I started feeding them, I got too close. And then you kept talking about turning them loose with the herd, and getting rid of the cattle, and I kept seeing their sad little faces and imagining how they would feel when they were stuffed into one of those big trucks and taken away to be killed. And I couldn't stand it, Troy. I had to do something."

"So you got your friends to smuggle them off the ranch in a 1987 converted van?"

"We thought a trailer might be too conspicuous."

"You had three calves running loose inside of Bobbi Jean Maxwell's vehicle?"

"Well, I put halters on them, but they were really hard to control."

He sat there for a moment, playing the mental video of the calves running amok in Bobbi Jean's van. He put his head on the desk.

"I'm sorry, Troy. I wrote you a note, and I was trying to find out how much the calves were worth so I could pay you. I wasn't stealing them."

"I know you weren't," he said, concentrating on the fake wood grain of the table.

"Please, don't be mad. I know you don't understand, but I had to save those calves. I couldn't live with myself. They would have haunted me forever."

"I know," he said again.

"Please, look at me! Please, don't make me beg."

He raised his head. "That depends on what you're begging for," he said with a smile.

"Troy! I'm serious. You can't be joking at a time like this."

"I didn't think I could, either, yet here I am, barely holding in uncontrollable laughter."

"What?"

He sputtered then, trying hard not to lose control. "The image of those calves inside the van. The idea that one of them was sitting in the front seat when the cop pulled Bobbi Jean over... You've got to admit it's pretty funny."

"It wasn't funny!"

"Maybe not then, but it is now."

"No, it's not! How can you laugh at me? I'm being charged with cattle rustling!"

"No, you're not. I'll fix it."

"I'm not sure you can," she said, her voice tentative. "Can you?"

"I think so. They're my cattle. You're my guest."

Just then there was a knock on the door. Chief Montoya came into the room. "All set?"

"Of course." Troy schooled his features into seriousness.

"Would you like to explain it to me?"

"I gave Ms. York responsibility for feeding and caring for the calves. They were orphans, and she looked on them as hers. So, when she got the opportunity to find them a home where they could live long, happy lives, she jumped on the chance to relocate them. Unfortunately, she chose a van instead of a trailer, but her intention was good."

"Did you know she was transporting the calves?"

He fudged his next answer a little. "I told her they could be moved."

"So she didn't steal them?"

"Of course not. It was a simple misunderstanding."

Chief Montoya looked at Troy for what seemed like forever, his face deadpan serious. Then he turned to Raven. "Don't ever move calves in vans again, young lady. I know you're not from around here, but you should have known better. I don't want to get a call where you've let one of them drive. Now get on out of here and don't be so secretive next time."

"Yes, sir. Are my friends free to go also?"

"They are."

"Thank you," Raven said.

"Thanks, Chief Montoya," Troy said, extending his hand. He and the police chief shook.

Raven stopped in the hallway. "I have to do something before I go back to the ranch."

"What now?"

"Well, two things, actually. I need to arrange for the calves to be moved, and I need to clean out Bobbi Jean's van."

"Why? Were the calves eating popcorn and drinking soda?"

"No, but one of them had a little accident. You see, I forgot they weren't housebroken. Bobbi Jean's sculpted shag carpet got a little messy, even with the painter's drop cloth."

Troy burst into laughter again.

BY THE TIME THEY ARRIVED BACK at the ranch, Raven had started to see the humor in the situation, while Troy had sobered a bit. They were rather quiet as he pulled the pickup to a stop near the house.

"Thank you again for arranging to transport the calves," she said.

"No problem. We couldn't leave them in police lockup, could we?"

"No, of course not." Raven opened the door and stepped outside. Clouds rolled in from the west and the air smelled like rain. She probably wasn't going to get any more work done outside today.

"Do you want to go to the café for dinner later?"

"No, I don't think I'm up to facing the citizens of

Brody's Crossing. If your town is anything like mine, news will travel fast."

"True. We don't have too many dangerous criminals running loose."

"I'm not dangerous."

He folded his arms and watched her, his eyes intent. "You were dangerous the other night."

She looked down at the dry ground and scrub grass. "That was different."

"Yes, it was, but I've decided I like different."

She looked up but couldn't read his expression.

"Why don't you get inside? I'm going to put the horses up. The sky looks like we're going to have a gully washer before long."

"Do you want me to help?"

"No, you might decide that the barn isn't comfortable enough and invite some of the horses into the house."

She frowned at him. "Not funny."

"I'm not joking."

She turned and stalked into the kitchen, but she heard Troy's laughter follow her until she shut the door.

She fixed some Earl Grey and a piece of toast since she'd forgotten to eat lunch. She really didn't want to think about her abortive attempt to rescue the calves, although they were now safe and secure at Bobbi Jean's small farm as they awaited a permanent home. And she especially didn't want to dwell on her night of passion with Troy, although now that he had brought it up, she could think of little else.

Just as she finished her toast, Troy entered along with a gust of damp wind. Outside, the trees bowed in the strong breeze, but Raven didn't see any raindrops yet. "Yep, we're going to get a downpour," he said, dusting off his hat and stomping his boots on the area rug.

"Would you like a hot drink?"

"Tea would be good."

She got up and went to the sink. "I didn't know you drank tea."

"I'd forgotten this until I saw you there, but my mother used to fix tea when one of us was coming down with a sore throat, or when the weather changed like this. She loved to watch storms."

Raven filled her mug and one for Troy. "Do you know what happened to your mother?"

"I found out a few years ago. She moved to Oregon after she left us, then to Seattle, then back to Oregon. Apparently she kept in touch with Ida Bell for a time. My mother knew, for example, that I'd graduated from college and moved to Fort Worth."

"That's good, but why didn't she ever contact you?"

"I guess because she was ashamed she left us. At least, that's what I think now. For years, I didn't know she cared about me. About us. And, quite frankly, she was never very interested in my father or my brother." He shrugged. "I was her favorite."

"It's so sad," Raven said, dunking tea bags in the hot water. "You missed so many years with her."

"Well, that was her choice."

"You didn't try to find her?"

He looked startled for a moment, then said, "I didn't know what name she was using."

So, he hadn't. Even more sad. If only one of them had reached out… But wasn't that so often the way?

She handed him a mug of tea, a spoon, and indicated

the honey she'd placed on the table. He chose white sugar instead.

"Okay, enough about me. I want to know something about you. Something I *need* to understand."

"Okay," she answered cautiously, taking her seat again.

He sat down across from her, just like in the police conference room. "Tell me why you love animals so much."

That wasn't the question she was expecting. She thought he was going to grill her again, ask her about moving the calves, or why she went behind his back. "Isn't it normal to love animals, especially baby ones?"

"Not like you do. When you first came here, I thought that you probably cared more for the beasts than you did for people. I realize now that's not true. But you have a special spot in your heart for animals, and I need to know where that comes from."

Raven took a deep breath. This wasn't something she wanted to talk about, but she owed Troy for not pressing charges, for making the "rustling" seem all a misunderstanding, for laughing at her when he could have been angry. "Like many of our beliefs, it goes back to what happened when I was a child."

"I'm listening."

"I'm the product of a single woman and a weekend fling. My mother likes to call it a brief relationship, but she never told me my father's name. On my birth certificate, the father is 'unknown.' I learned his name later, but I have no contact with him—his choice."

She paused and squirmed in the chair. "We grew up poor. My grandparents didn't approve of my mother getting pregnant and deciding to keep the child. They aren't the warm-and-friendly type. More often than not, my mother and

I depended on the kindness of friends, and occasionally on the charity of strangers. I grew up with hand-me-down-down-downs. I had lunch coupons at school. We sometimes had Thanksgiving at the local church, with homeless and destitute families. I know what it's like to be unwanted."

"I'm sorry."

She nodded. "I loved animals, but we didn't have enough money to feed ourselves, much less a pet. I volunteered at the local animal shelter, walking dogs and grooming cats. I tried to find them all homes. Sometimes I couldn't, and I cried." She took a deep breath. "I wanted that perfect ending for everyone, the ending I never saw for myself. I think I transferred all my love and hopes and affection to animals."

"Ah, that explains so much."

"I've thought about it a lot. I now understand why I love animals, but that doesn't mean I care about them any less." She looked down at her mug, feeling her eyes well with tears she didn't want to shed. "Every time I see an animal that is unloved or unwanted, I see myself as a little girl, and all the feelings come back. I wish I could stop it, but I don't know how. I don't even know if I want to. I think those feelings make me who I am now, and if I'm not that person, who would I be?"

Troy reached across the table and took her hand. "I'll tell you who you are. You are the most compassionate, caring woman I think I've ever met. You might have been unwanted and even unloved as a child, although I find that hard to believe, but as an adult, you are far from unwanted. Everyone who meets you loves…or at least appreciates you. You make friends everywhere. All the people I talk to in town ask about you. They smile when they think of you, Raven, and that says a lot."

She used her other hand to grab a napkin and wipe her eyes. She sniffed, trying hard not to give in to a crying binge when all she really wanted was to curl up against Troy's broad chest and let him hold her while she let loose.

He knew her better than almost anyone. He made her laugh and cry and...oh my God. She was in love in with him.

"We're going to look after your calves, Raven," he said, as if she hadn't just had the most remarkable revelation in her life. "I don't know where they'll end up, but we'll find a place. You've already saved Riley. Who knows what else you'll accomplish before you go back to New Hampshire."

She nodded, too stunned to make conversation. "Yes, who knows," she whispered. But she didn't think she'd accomplish all that much more. Her work on the garden would be finished in a few days. There was nothing else to do but pack up and go home.

She couldn't very well blurt out that she was in love with Troy Crawford and wanted to be with him forever.

THAT NIGHT AS HE SAT AT THE desk Troy thought about what Raven had told him for a long time. She'd had an even rougher childhood than he had. Although his mother had left him, she'd loved him—he couldn't deny that she had, at least while he was a child—and had taken care of him. He hadn't worn old clothes or worried about their next meal. Although ranch life wasn't always prosperous, they'd had a place to live and a heritage he hadn't appreciated.

Raven had no relationship with her father, had a mother who'd grudgingly looked after her, and had always felt lacking. Yet she'd grown up to be a kind, compassionate and caring person. True, she could be irritating with her animal-rights beliefs, but they were important to her, and now that he understood them, he felt a little more sympathetic.

But where did that leave him? He still had to put final touches on a strategy to save the ranch. He had to get bank approval for the new business plan and contact potential collaborators. And finally, those cattle had to be sent off to the slaughterhouse.

He'd wait until Raven left to do that, no matter what the price of beef was at the moment. He couldn't have her watch them get loaded into trailers. But what else could he do? They were steers, not breeding stock. He couldn't afford to feed them, pure and simple. It was kinder to sell them now while grass and water were still plentiful.

He thought about when he was a child, when there was a meat market and butcher here in town. What had happened to old Mr. Chemenski? He'd spoken with a thick foreign accent and always wore a white apron in his shop. Troy remembered going in there with his mother. The store was filled with all cuts of beef and pork, plus chicken and some more exotic choices. He'd even carried rattlesnake after the annual roundup. They'd tried it once; it was full of bones, but did taste a little like chicken.

Too bad there wasn't a meat market in town now. Perhaps he'd see about keeping at least some of the cattle for the local market. On a whim, he added that to his list.

A knock on the door startled him. Raven stood there. "I'm getting ready for bed, and before I turned in, I wanted to thank you again. I know you're going through a lot, and I didn't mean to add to your problems."

He stood up and stretched. "You didn't. You gave me a nice jolt in the middle of the day. We don't get many cattle rustlers around here, although it's not unheard of. Usually, they come with big trailers, not eighties vans."

She ignored his attempt at humor. "I also wanted to tell you that I'll probably be finished by Sunday. I'll transfer some of the plants to Ida, who's fostering them until we hear back on what species I found, and the availability of seeds or plants, and get my final report on the garden ready to mail to Mrs. Philpot. She documents every plant species found on homesteads."

He took a deep breath, looking at her closely. She'd dressed in jeans and a simple T-shirt, and her feet were bare. Her face was composed, free of makeup or joyous smiles, and her glorious hair was brushed and slightly subdued, much like her mood tonight.

"Raven, I—" A jolt of thunder made them both jump. "The storm is finally here," he said unnecessarily.

She hugged her arms around her middle. "This is the first since I got here."

"Do you want to stand outside and watch it rain?"

"I…I suppose."

"Come on." He impulsively took her hand and led her to the front door. Riley followed.

The rain came down in sheets, although it was so dark it was difficult to see in the weak glow of the single outdoor porch light. An occasional flash of lightning to the south threw the clouds into sharp relief and showed the thunderstorm in its full glory.

Riley whined and went back inside. Raven smiled, and Troy stepped closer. "He doesn't appreciate how much we need this rain."

"No, but I kind of like it."

"Me, too. I've always liked storms." He put his arm

around Raven, pulling her close to his side. "You know what's really nice on a night like this?"

"Hot tea and carob-chip scones?"

"Er, no." He didn't even want to imagine what carob-chip scones would taste like. "No, I was thinking more about snuggling together in a nice soft bed."

"Really? I didn't know that."

"Trust me, it's great."

"I don't know…"

"You should try it."

"With you?"

"I'm a good teacher."

She turned to face him, looking up with dark eyes that searched his. "I remember that about you."

He kissed her then, their breath merging and their bodies melting together. Hunger rose, hot and heavy, and he hardened even as she softened in response. He ran his hands down her back, holding her close. He remembered her slim, firm body and her just-right curves. He longed to feel them again, without layers of clothes in the way.

"I wish we could make love outside," she whispered.

"I'm game if you are," he offered, kissing her neck.

"This is a little too open."

"No one will be by in this weather."

"Still, I think I'd like to learn about this snuggling in a nice soft bed with the storm outside."

"Okay. Maybe next time," he said lightly, but he realized there might not be a "next time," and she knew it, too. The end of her stay on the Rocking C was in sight, and that lent a melancholy air to the night that complemented the weather. "Let's go inside. I'll open the window and we'll listen to the rain."

She nodded and took his offered hand. "Let's go."

They made love as if it truly were the last time, whether it was or not. And then Troy held her all night.

When he awoke the next morning, she was still beside him, and he smiled.

Chapter Fifteen

Troy had asked her to stay until Tuesday, and Raven agreed. What difference did one or two days make? She could mail her report from Brody's Crossing on Monday and see her friends for lunch. He had an appointment with the banker, which apparently had met with the "committee" on the new business plan Troy had presented on Friday.

The last few days had proven that she really was in love with Troy. She hadn't said the words, although they'd been on the tip of her tongue more than once. In the height of passion or in the peaceful aftermath, she felt affection for this man, who was so different from anyone she'd ever known. So different from her. There was no future for two such disparate people. Couples who had far more in common still broke up.

She and Troy did share two important things, though. Both had had tumultuous relationships with their mothers. Both of them were torn in their feelings for family. Raven loved her mother because she'd done the best she could, but they weren't close. Troy's had left him, which he'd never forgotten nor forgiven. Her desertion and his father's criticism had defined Troy as a man. Raven knew how hard the past was to overcome, but she hoped that the letters she'd found, plus the copy of the letter Troy's mother had sent the garden society and that Mrs. Philpot had returned would help. She would leave those for him when she went back to New Hampshire tomorrow morning.

Today, she would have lunch with her fellow rustlers. She'd called to make sure they would be at the café, since she had to bring the plants she was leaving with Ida. She pulled Pickles into a slot in the vacant lot next to the café. Ahead of her, the old hotel still stood. Beside that, the now unused railroad tracks remained. The small depot could have been used for some purpose but was also empty. This town had suffered, but it had survived change. Much like a garden, the toughest endured.

Raven carefully carried the plants and a few good-bye gifts for her friends into the café. As soon as she opened the door, the whole place erupted in "Surprise!" Raven nearly dropped her precious cargo as everyone rushed forward.

"We wanted to give you a proper send-off," Clarissa said, her eyes alight with joy.

"We are going to miss you so much," Ida Bell said, hugging Raven.

"Even when I get you in trouble with the law?" Raven asked, feeling her eyes moisten.

"Even then," Bobbi Jean answered, stepping up to kiss her also.

"You shouldn't have," Raven said, wiping away tears.

The smiling produce manager, whom Raven didn't know by name, said, "You have a way of shaking things up good."

"I'm sure that with your suggestions, we'll get the old farmers' market open again," another person called from farther back in the café.

"And you know all the best natural cures, so we don't have to take a bunch of prescription drugs," someone added.

Raven scrubbed at her eyes again. "Stop, please. You're making me blush and cry at the same time!"

They laughed, and Raven was guided to a table in the middle. "Maybe we'll just keep you here," Ida joked. Raven sobered a little, although she kept her smile in place. Only one person could make her think about staying, and even that wasn't going to work. She just didn't belong in Texas permanently. She had a home and a life waiting.

TROY PARKED THE TRUCK BY THE back door, relieved to see Raven's green Volvo parked there. He knew she'd been to town for lunch. Ida had called him to tell him about the surprise party. Her friend was checking to make sure Raven was coming into town. She also wanted to see if there was any way he could make her stay in Brody's Crossing for good.

That wasn't his decision to make, he'd told Ida. Then he'd realized that they'd never discussed her staying. She'd always been firm that she needed to get back to New Hampshire. She'd never said she didn't want to go.

But maybe he should have asked. Maybe, when he was buried deep inside her, he could have mentioned he wanted her with him more than anything. Maybe he could have told her one more time how much he'd enjoyed having her at the ranch, even when she did aggravate him. He hadn't done either of those things, and tomorrow she was leaving.

He tried to tell himself that it was for the best, that she wouldn't want to be on a cattle ranch for however long he was here. Even when he finally left the Rocking C, he'd still be involved in the beef industry. He couldn't imagine Raven living in his Fort Worth condo.

His building didn't allow bunnies, goats and sheep. Hell, it even had a rule limiting the size of dogs. Riley was too big. Troy didn't even know what she wanted to do with the dog.

He kind of liked Riley.

He unloaded his briefcase, which seemed a little formal with his jeans and western shirt. However, that's what he'd needed for the bank paperwork and business plan. Pushing open the back door, he walked inside and laid it on the kitchen table.

"Raven?" He didn't hear her, but in a moment, Riley walked slowly out of her bedroom, barely wagging his tail. Troy scratched the dog's head as he passed by.

"I'm packing," she said, stuffing things into her canvas tote bag. "You should see the nice things my friends gave me. Homemade candles and soap. Some Texas bluebonnet seeds. They were so thoughtful." Her words sounded reasonable, but the tone was all wrong.

"Don't go," he said, surprising himself. Surprising her. She froze, then turned to face him.

"I have to go home."

"Can you stay longer? Can you—"

"No, I can't." She turned back to her packing.

He stood there for a moment, watching her, then said, "When you get finished, would you like to see what I'm going to do with the ranch? I have the response back from the bank."

"Of course. Let me finish this and I'll be right there."

He left her before he said something else stupid. Like, *Don't go. Ever. Stay with me. I need you.*

No, he wasn't going to say any of that. She didn't want

to hear it, and he didn't have any business asking. He'd be the worst match in the world for a homebody like Raven. He didn't know how to make a commitment, and even if he did, he'd probably be like his mother and run off. Didn't everyone say he was more like her than his dad?

A few minutes later she came into the kitchen. He'd opened the briefcase and was sorting through papers.

"Well, I listened to you and my friends. I listened to experts I'd never met before and I read lots of opinions and facts. The one person I didn't talk to is my brother, which means he's probably going to have a fit when he gets home. But it's my decision, and before I reveal it, I want to tell you something else."

"What?"

"For many years I blamed my family for my unhappiness. When I succeeded, I felt as if I was saying 'that'll show you.' When they screwed up, I wanted to shout 'I told you so.' No matter how far I went or what I did, I was tied to this ranch. It defined me."

Raven nodded, her expression intent, and he continued. "I wasn't being fair to them or to myself. I'd never moved on. Unlike you, who'd really thought about how your childhood affected you, I pushed it aside. I was critical of my father, then my brother, because they didn't listen to my ideas. Then I realized that, once I became a man, I never attempted to help my brother as an equal, as an adult. I watched him failing and I didn't do anything, and that was wrong."

"But he was running the ranch. From what you said, he wouldn't have listened."

"Probably, but the point is, I didn't even try. I might not have mentioned this, but this ranch is forty-nine percent mine. My brother has controlling interest, but my father left it to me, too. He didn't cut me out, even though I wouldn't let him or my brother be a part of my adult life. Just like my mother cut us all out of hers."

"Oh, Troy, I think you're being too hard on yourself."

"No, I think I'm finally being honest with myself. And because of that, I'm going to save the Rocking C, just in case my brother ever gets around to producing another generation to pass it to."

"Or you do," she said softly.

"Yeah, that might be a distant possibility, but I haven't had much luck."

"Maybe you haven't asked the right person. Or the right question."

He looked at her hard for a moment, then glanced away. "We can talk more about that comment later. For now, let me show you what the Rocking C will become."

He laid out a map. "I'm dividing the land into different functions. You reminded me of the importance of diversification when you talked about your farm. Here," he said, pointing to a large section of land, "will be the pasture for the dairy cattle. We're going organic—"

"Oh, Troy, how wonderful!"

"I know, but don't get too excited yet." He indicated another area. "This smaller pasture is hilly with some rocky ground, which isn't good for cattle. It's going to be subleased to a farmer who is interested in free-range chickens. He's going to raise laying hens and sell eggs."

"Again, that's terrific."

"This section is the most level and easiest to irrigate. I'm going to plant our own hay fields. It's something I've always wanted to do for the ranch."

"That's good."

"Now, the last part you're not going to like, but we need the revenue. The largest area of land here will be used for natural beef and bison. I'm getting bison from a ranch in Oklahoma. There's a small but steady demand for their meat and there's a growing need for certified organic beef in places like Whole Foods Market."

She sat there silently. Finally she asked, "You can't send organically raised cattle and bison off to the stock-yards, can you?"

"No. I've talked to the butcher who used to be in town. He's retired, but his grandson wants to reopen the shop. He already has an Internet business, so he's got an idea to base his operations here in Brody's Crossing and ship organic meat all around the country."

"Wow. I'm impressed. Not that I'm for killing the cattle, of course."

"At least they'll be raised organically. And, sure, they'll be killed, but it won't be the same kind of death they'd face in a slaughterhouse. New business is something this town needs. It's a change for the better."

"You're right, of course," she said just a little reluctantly.

"The bank has approved all the changes. I'll continue to look for other ideas, but this ranch is moving on."

"Doesn't your brother have to say yes to all this first?"

"Not since he gave me power of attorney."

She looked at him for a moment, then smiled. "I'm happy for you, Troy. Really, I am."

"I want to keep Riley," he said, so he wouldn't blurt out something even more stupid than he had earlier. "At least for now. When I go back to Fort Worth, I'll contact you. I can't take him to my condo. He wouldn't be happy anyway."

"Oh." Her face fell, then she nodded. "You're right. He loves it here, and he's crazy about you."

I'm crazy about you, he wanted to say, but didn't. As the silence grew uncomfortable, the phone rang.

"I'd better get that. I'm waiting for an important call." She pushed away from the table and rushed to the office. Troy folded his map.

He'd done it. He'd come up with a workable plan for the ranch. He felt relief and a healthy dose of fear. What if it didn't fly?

If it didn't, he'd modify it. He'd put his own money into the ranch. He wouldn't let the Rocking C fail, even if his strategy needed to be revised. He wouldn't be like his father and brother, who decided on one thing and believed it would be successful despite all evidence to the contrary.

Raven came back into the room, a smile lighting up her face. "I've found a home for the calves. A farm that has corporate parties and attracts tourists to its 'real West' environment wants them. They'll be in the petting zoo this summer, then they'll be part of the small herd they have there. They've promised me that the calves will be safe, and they'll sign a paper that if they ever don't have room for them, they'll give me the chance to move them."

"That's great," he said, smiling up at her. "Should I make arrangements to have them shipped?"

"I think so…that is, if it's not too much trouble."

"No, it's not." At the moment, with the ranch settled and his feelings about his family more sorted out, he'd do almost anything to help Raven.

RAVEN FINISHED ALL HER PACKING except for the clothes she'd wear tomorrow and her few toiletries. Earlier she'd carefully placed the old spinning wheel in the back of Pickles so it wouldn't get damaged on the long drive. She knew she'd never refinish it, but because Troy had cleaned it for her, she would use it and think of him.

She left the canvas bag open just in case she forgot something. Closing it seemed way too...final.

She needed to pay one last visit to the barn, to look around and say good-bye to the horses. She wanted to spend some time with Riley, to explain that she had to go back to New Hampshire. She needed...she wasn't sure, but felt something was wrong. Something seemed to be missing.

"Do you want to go to Dewey's and get a bite to eat?" Troy asked when she walked into the living room. He hadn't changed out of his nicer Wranglers and shirt.

"I suppose." She felt listless. "I don't feel hungry, but I think I need to eat."

They went in Troy's SUV. There was no live band on Monday night, so they ate to the sound of the jukebox in the background. Troy nodded to several people Raven didn't know. She drank a glass of iced tea because ordering a beer might seem as if she were celebrating her departure. Or drinking because she was depressed about leaving.

As Troy drove back to the ranch, she listened to a sad country-and-western song on the radio. Why were cowboys so gloomy? She'd hardly ever heard a happy song. "I won't miss the music," she said out loud.

"You won't?" He drove around a turn, then asked, "What will you miss?"

You. I'll miss you for a long, long time. Like forever, she wanted to say, but didn't. "I'll miss the almost constant sunshine. I'll miss the horses and the calves, of course, and

Riley. He's a good dog. I can't imagine why someone didn't want him."

"Maybe he was meant to be here, on this ranch. Maybe it was destiny that you were driving on that road and found him. Did you think about that?"

"No." He'd mentioned something like this before, about fate playing a role in her ending up in Texas. "Do you think that the assignment mix-up was destiny? Was that a good thing?"

"I think so. Don't you? Or do you wish you'd never come here?"

"No, I don't wish that at all. I'll never regret spending these weeks on the Rocking C."

He pulled the SUV to a stop. Raven was surprised that they were back at the house already. He unhooked his seat belt and turned slightly to her. "Stay with me tonight."

She nodded. One last night. He hadn't asked her not to go, so it must be time to leave. She'd settled for second best and hand-me-downs too often in her life; she wasn't going to settle for a halfhearted request that she stay just a little longer. What difference would that make?

In the end, she'd still head back to New Hampshire, and she'd know that she wasn't enough—good enough, beautiful enough, compatible enough—for him to love.

THE NEXT MORNING, RAVEN MADE coffee while Troy did chores. She fed Riley, talking to him about the evils of eating meat, even if Troy did keep giving it to him. She put her last items in her bag, closed it up and put it beside the back door. She cleaned out the refrigerator, sure that Troy didn't want any of her leftovers, and packed her cooler with goat cheese, fruit, tofu and bottled water.

In the office she'd left the letters from his mother that she'd found in one of the boxes, plus the one forwarded by Mrs. Philpot. They proved how much Luanna Crawford had loved this ranch and her sons, but couldn't live with the increasing criticism and lack of understanding from her husband. She left the boys here because Cal was already grown, and Troy needed the stability of his home.

"I'm as ready as I'm going to be," she told Riley, who watched her suspiciously, as if he knew what the tote bag and cooler meant. She knelt down and put her arms around him. "I'll miss you so much. You behave for Troy. Learn to be a good cattle dog. No chasing the chickens."

She got up from the floor just as Troy came in the back door. "Hey," he said.

"Hey to you," she said, forcing a smile. "I'm all packed. I think I'll go ahead and get on the road."

Troy frowned. "Don't you want breakfast?"

"I'll get something on the way."

"What if you can't find anything organic?"

"I'll be fine. It won't kill me to eat a bagel or get a regular scrambled egg."

"I'll fix you something."

"No, really," she said, knowing if she stayed she'd turn into a big crybaby again. "I think I should leave."

"No."

"Troy, I can't stay any longer. I have to get home to my farm. Besides, you're going to be really busy here. Just think of all the improvements you need to make. Why, you won't even miss me."

"I think I'll miss you forever. I'm missing you already, and you haven't gone yet."

She put up a hand. "Please, don't do this to me."

"I tried. I wasn't going to say anything. I was going to be strong. But dammit, Raven, I can't just watch you walk away."

"Then don't watch. Stay here. I'll just go, and we'll promise to keep in touch, and that way I won't cry."

"Don't cry."

"I won't." Not until she was on the road, at least.

"I'm terrible at relationships. I just figured out where I went wrong with my brother and father. I never did get over my mother leaving. I've never been in love or asked anyone to move in with me, much less anything more serious."

"Troy, you don't need to tell me this. Either you…feel a certain way about me, or you don't."

"No, it's not that simple. I'm trying to tell you that you should be glad to get away from here, even if I selfishly want you to stay. I'm a bad risk when it comes to romance."

She stood there in the kitchen, knowing she couldn't *tell* Troy anything. Either he saw the truth, or he didn't. Riley even came over and whined, as if he was sympathetic to the humans' star-crossed situation.

Raven picked up her tote bag. "I can't believe you're so afraid of love."

"It's not about fear."

"Of course it is. You're afraid to love because your mother left you. I know how that feels because at one time, I was scared, too. I didn't feel lovable because of my mother. But then I learned that it's better to feel, to love. It beats cutting yourself off from people."

"I'm a grown man. I'm not hiding behind my mother's desertion." He grabbed Raven's bag from her. "I'm just being realistic. Besides, when did you ever say you wanted to stay? I don't remember us having that conversation."

"Stay?" She turned to face him at the back door. "I

don't want to stay on the Rocking C. As you've pointed out many times, it's not my home. It's not even your home. Yet you're here."

"Temporarily. Until my brother comes back."

"And then where will you be?"

"In Fort Worth. Or wherever else I want to go. Once I'm finished here, I can decide."

She looked up at Troy, knowing she loved him but not willing to ask for anything he wasn't able to give. "Then why would you ask me to stay on this ranch, even for a little while longer, as if it were my home? It's not a forever kind of place for me. It's not my heritage."

She pushed open the back door while she could still use hurt and anger as a shield. She was such a crybaby lately. But feeling meant emotional pain along with joy, so she couldn't deny that side of herself, any more than she could deny that she loved Troy.

"You know more than anyone that this ranch is part of me."

"Yes, I do." She put her tote on Pickles's front seat. "But it's not all of you. It's not the best part of you."

"What is?"

She paused for a moment, then said, "Your goodness. You're a good man, Troy Crawford, and you don't give yourself enough credit for how much you care about others."

He reached for her arm. "Don't go."

She looked up into his face with its tight-set lips and furrowed brow. So many emotions flickered in his eyes. But he said nothing more, and she turned away.

She put the cooler in the floor of the back seat, then turned around to close the door.

He stepped in front of her. "Don't go," Troy said again, "because I love you."

She stopped and watched him, her heart beating hard. "That's a good start."

He took a deep breath. "Don't go, because my home is where you are, not on this ranch or in Fort Worth. I don't know why I didn't see that before. I never thought…and yet, it's so simple." He smiled, and it was as if the clouds parted after days of gloom. "I love you more than I want to be anyplace, more than I want to do anything. Without you, my life will be empty. Again. And I don't think I could stand being alone after knowing and loving you."

She felt tears of joy just before she launched herself into his arms. "See? Was that so hard to say?"

"Not hard to say," he said, burying his head against her neck, "but damn hard to realize."

She laughed despite her tears, and he laughed and swung her in a circle. Her gauzy skirt floated around them, her scarf wrapped them up tight, and still he laughed and twirled until they were both dizzy and falling against Pickles. Riley barked and jumped up and down in glee.

"I love you, Troy Crawford, with all my heart, like I never imagined I could love a Texas cowboy."

"I'm not really a cowboy," he said, resting his forehead against hers, "and maybe we won't end up in Texas. But please, darlin', don't expect me to learn to love tofu and goat cheese."

She tilted her head and smiled. "I promise I'll take real good care of you."

"That's what I was afraid of," he said just before he kissed her.

Epilogue

July 2007

Troy watched the dairy cows walk down the ramp from the trailer, their big bellies and full udders swaying. The refurbished barn, with its new milking equipment, gleamed with a coat of bright red paint.

Raven had insisted that there be no more gray or beige on the Rocking C. Troy smiled at the memory, and wondered how his brother would react to all the changes. The bricks on the ranch house had been pressure washed and she was busy painting the trim a sedate but strong green. The rooms inside had been cleaned and decorated, and they'd replaced some of the outdated appliances. They weren't sure when Cal would come home, but they thought it would be before Christmas. That was good, because Raven was dividing her time between her farm and the ranch. Besides, they couldn't plan the wedding until they knew when they'd be moving.

Troy had quit his job as the marketing director for Devboran cattle, and he would look for a new position after they settled in New Hampshire. Raven was hoping he'd find something promoting organic produce, while he'd be happy with a job that produced a different kind of green—cash.

He'd sunk a lot into the Rocking C and would like to see a return on his investment. But he also wanted to support his bride in the style she'd never known. They would need a bigger house if they were going to work on the next Crawford generation. They'd been practicing—a lot!

"Aren't they beautiful?" she asked as she stopped beside him and rested her arms on the fence.

"They're different from Herefords, that's for sure."

"Poor Herefords. Do you think they're in cow heaven, looking down on us and wishing us well?"

"I think that might be stretching it."

"At least the three calves are safe."

"We can go visit them in a couple of weeks, once we get the bison settled in."

"I can't believe all we've done," she said, looking around.

"There's just one more thing," he said, looking down at Raven's glossy hair. "You need a proper hat."

She put her hand on her head. "The sun is awfully hot."

"Right. How about we go to Fort Worth this weekend and I take you shopping? I promise that no beavers or any other animals will be killed in the making of your hat."

Raven laughed. "Sounds good. I can go to the natural-foods store. I need to stock up."

Troy groaned. "No more tofu."

"Don't be so grumpy," she said, pulling out of his grasp and twirling away with a teasing smile. "I found a new recipe I just know you'll love."

Troy grinned as he watched her walk away. He'd try just about anything to make his swirly-girly Yankee fiancée happy. Well, anything but tofu and goat cheese together.

* * * * *

*Look for Victoria Chancellor's next book
in the Brody's Crossing series,
TEXAN FOR THE HOLIDAYS,
coming in December 2007,
only from Harlequin American Romance!*

**Every Life Has More
Than One Chapter**™

Award-winning author Stevi Mittman delivers
another hysterical mystery, featuring Teddi Bayer, an
irrepressible heroine, and her to-die-for hero, Detective Drew Scoones. After all, life on Long Island can
be murder!

*Turn the page for a sneak peek at the warm
and funny fourth book,
WHOSE NUMBER IS UP, ANYWAY?,
in the Teddi Bayer series,
by STEVI MITTMAN.
On sale August 7*

"Before redecorating a room, I always advise my clients to empty it of everything but one chair. Then I suggest they move that chair from place to place, sitting in it, until the placement feels right. Trust your instincts when deciding on furniture placement. Your room should 'feel right.'"

—TipsFromTeddi.com

Gut feelings. You know, that gnawing in the pit of your stomach that warns you that you are about to do the absolute stupidest thing you could do? Something that will ruin life as you know it?

I've got one now, standing at the butcher counter in King Kullen, the grocery store in the same strip mall as L.I. Lanes, the bowling alley-cum-billiard parlor I'm in the process of redecorating for its "Grand Opening."

I realize being in the wrong supermarket probably doesn't sound exactly dire to you, but you aren't the one buying your father a brisket at a store your mother will somehow know isn't Waldbaum's.

And then, June Bayer isn't your mother.

The woman behind the counter has agreed to go into the freezer to find a brisket for me, since there aren't any in the case. There are packages of pork tenderloin, piles of spareribs and rolls of sausage, but no briskets.

Warning Number Two, right? I should be so out of here.

But no, I'm still in the same spot when she comes back out, brisketless, her face ashen. She opens her mouth as if she is going to scream, but only a gurgle comes out.

And then she pinballs out from behind the counter, knocking bottles of Peter Luger Steak Sauce to the floor on her way, now hitting the tower of cans at the end of the prepared foods aisle and sending them sprawling, now making her way down the aisle, careening from side to side as she goes.

Finally, from a distance, I hear her shout, "He's deeeeeeaaaad! Joey's deeeeeaaaad."

My first thought is *You should always trust your gut.*

My second thought is that now, somehow, my mother will know I was in King Kullen. For weeks I will have to hear "What did you expect?" as though whenever you go to King Kullen someone turns up dead. And if the detective investigating the case turns out to be Detective Drew Scoones… well, I'll never hear the end of that from her, either.

She still suspects I murdered the guy who was found dead on my doorstep last Halloween just to get Drew back into my life.

Several people head for the butcher's freezer and I position myself to block them. If there's one thing I've learned from finding people dead—and the guy on my doorstep wasn't the first one—it's that the police get very testy when you mess with their murder scenes.

"You can't go in there until the police get here," I say, stationing myself at the end of the butcher's counter and in front of the Employees Only door, acting as if I'm some sort of authority. "You'll contaminate the evidence if it turns out to be murder."

Shouts and chaos. You'd think I'd know better than to throw the word *murder* around. Cell phones are flipping open and tongues are wagging.

I amend my statement quickly. "Which, of course, it probably isn't. Murder, I mean. People die all the time, and it's not always in hospitals or their own beds, or…" I babble when I'm nervous, and the idea of someone dead on the other side of the freezer door makes me very nervous.

So does the idea of seeing Drew Scoones again. Drew and I have this on-again, off-again sort of thing…that I kind of turned off.

Who knew he'd take it so personally when he tried to get serious and I responded by saying we could talk about *us* tomorrow—and then caught a plane to my parents' condo in Boca the next day? In July. In the middle of a job.

For some crazy reason, he took that to mean that I was avoiding him and the subject of *us*.

That was three months ago. I haven't seen him since.

The manager, who identifies himself and points to his nameplate in case I don't believe him, says he has to go into *his cooler.* "Maybe Joey's not dead," he says. "Maybe he can be saved, and you're letting him die in there. Did you ever think of that?"

In fact, I hadn't. But I had thought that the murderer

might try to go back in to make sure his tracks were covered, so I say that I will go in and check.

Which means that the manager and I couple up and go in together while everyone pushes against the doorway to peer in, erasing any chance of finding clean prints on that Employees Only door.

I expect to find carcasses of dead animals hanging from hooks, and maybe Joey hanging from one, too. I think it's going to be very creepy and I steel myself, only to find a rather benign series of shelves with large slabs of meat laid out carefully on them, along with boxes and boxes marked simply Chicken.

Nothing scary here, unless you count the body of a middle-aged man with graying hair sprawled faceup on the floor. His eyes are wide open and unblinking. His shirt is stiff. His pants are stiff. His body is stiff. And his expression, you should forgive the pun—is frozen. Bill-the-manager crosses himself and stands mute while I pronounce the guy dead in a sort of *happy now?* tone.

"We should not be in here," I say, and he nods his head emphatically and helps me push people out of the doorway just in time to hear the police sirens and see the cop cars pull up outside the big store windows.

Bobbie Lyons, my partner in Teddi Bayer Interior Designs (and also my neighbor, my best friend and my private fashion police), and Mark, our carpenter (and my dogsitter, confidant, and ego booster), rush in from next door. They beat the cops by a half step and shout out my name. People point in my direction.

After all the publicity that followed the unfortunate incident during which I shot my ex-husband, Rio Gallo, and then the subsequent murder of my first client—which

I solved, I might add—it seems like the whole world, or at least all of Long Island, knows who I am.

Mark asks if I'm all right. (Did I remember to mention that the man is drop-dead-gorgeous-but-a-decade-too-young-for-me-yet-too-old-for-my-daughter-thank-god?) I don't get a chance to answer him because the police are quickly closing in on the store manager and me.

"The woman—" I begin telling the police. Then I have to pause for the manager to fill in her name, which he does: *Fran.*

I continue. "Right. Fran. Fran went into the freezer to get a brisket. A moment later she came out and screamed that Joey was dead. So I'd say she was the one who discovered the body."

"And you are…?" the cop asks me. It comes out a bit like who do I *think* I am, rather than who am I really?

"An innocent bystander," Bobbie, hair perfect, makeup just right, says, carefully placing her body between the cop and me.

"And she was just leaving," Mark adds. They each take one of my arms.

Fran comes into the inner circle surrounding the cops. In case it isn't obvious from the hairnet and bloodstained white apron with Fran embroidered on it, I explain that she was the butcher who was going for the brisket. Mark and Bobbie take that as a signal that I've done my job and they can now get me out of there. They twist around, with me in the middle, as if we're a Rockettes line, until we are facing away from the butcher counter. They've managed to propel me a few steps toward the exit when disaster—in the form of a Mazda RX7 pulling up at the loading curb—strikes.

Mark's grip on my arm tightens like a vise. "Too late," he says.

Bobbie's expletive is unprintable. "Maybe there's a back door," she suggests, but Mark is right. It's too late.

I've laid my eyes on Detective Scoones. And while my gut is trying to warn me that my heart shouldn't go there, regions farther south are melting at just the sight of him.

"Walk," Bobbie orders me.

And I try to. Really.

Walk, I tell my feet. *Just put one foot in front of the other.*

I can do this because I know, in my heart of hearts, that if Drew Scoones was still interested in me, he'd have gotten in touch with me after I returned from Boca. And he didn't.

Since he's a detective, Drew doesn't have to wear one of those dark blue Nassau County Police uniforms. Instead, he's got on jeans, a tight-fitting T-shirt and a tweedy sports jacket. If you think that sounds good, you should see him. Chiseled features, cleft chin, brown hair that's naturally a little sandy in the front, a smile that…well, that doesn't matter. He isn't smiling now.

He walks up to me, tucks his sunglasses into his breast pocket and looks me over from head to toe.

"Well, if it isn't Miss Cut and Run," he says. "Aren't you supposed to be somewhere in Florida or something?" He looks at Mark accusingly, as if he was covering for me when he told Drew I was gone.

"Detective Scoones?" one of the uniforms says. "The stiff's in the cooler and the woman who found him is over there." He jerks his head in Fran's direction.

Drew continues to stare at me.

You know how when you were young, your mother

always told you to wear clean underwear in case you were in an accident? And how, a little further on, she told you not to go out in hair rollers because you never knew who you might see—or who might see you? And how now your best friend says she wouldn't be caught dead without makeup and suggests you shouldn't either?

Okay, today, *finally,* in my overalls and Converse sneakers, I get it.

I brush my hair out of my eyes. "Well, I'm back," I say. As if he hasn't known my exact whereabouts. The man is a detective, for heaven's sake. "Been back awhile."

Bobbie has watched the exchange and apparently decided she's given Drew all the time he deserves. "And we've got work to do, so…" she says, grabbing my arm and giving Drew a little two-fingered wave good-bye.

As I back up a foot or two, the store manager sees his chance and places himself in front of Drew, trying to get his attention. Maybe what makes Drew such a good detective is his ability to focus.

Only what he's focusing on is me.

"Phone broken? Carrier pigeon died?" he asks me, taking in Fran, the manager, the meat counter and that Employees Only door, all without taking his eyes off me.

Mark tries to break the spell. "We've got work to do there, you've got work to do here, Scoones," Mark says to him, gesturing toward next door. "So it's back to the alley for us."

Drew's lip twitches. "You working the alley now?" he says.

"If you'd like to follow me," Bill-the-manager, clearly exasperated, says to Drew—who doesn't respond. It's as if waiting for my answer is all he has to do.

So, fine. "You knew I was back," I say.

The man has known my whereabouts every hour of the day for as long as I've known him. And my mother's not the only one who won't buy that he "just happened" to answer this particular call. In fact, I'm willing to bet my children's lunch money that he's taken every call within ten miles of my home since the day I got back.

And now he's gotten lucky.

"*You* could have called *me,*" I say.

"You're the one who said *tomorrow* for our talk and then flew the coop, chickie," he says. "I figured the ball was in your court."

"Detective?" the uniform says. "There's something you ought to see in here."

Drew gives me a look that amounts to *in or out?*

He could be talking about the investigation, or about our relationship.

Bobbie tries to steer me away. Mark's fists are balled. Drew waits me out, knowing I won't be able to resist what might be a murder investigation.

Finally he turns and heads for the cooler.

And, like a puppy dog, I follow.

Bobbie grabs the back of my shirt and pulls me to a halt.

"I'm just going to show him something," I say, yanking away.

"Yeah," Bobbie says, pointedly looking at the buttons on my blouse. The two at breast level have popped. "That's what I'm afraid of."

HARLEQUIN®

Super Romance®

*Looking for a romantic, emotional
and unforgettable escape?*

*You'll find it this month and every month
with a Harlequin Superromance!*

Rory Gorenzi has a sense of humor and a sense of
honor. She also happens to be good with children.

Seamus Lee, widower and father of four, needs
someone with exactly those traits.

They meet at the Colorado mountain school owned
by Rory's father, where she teaches skiing and
avalanche safety. But Seamus—and his children—
learn more from her than that....

Look for

GOOD WITH CHILDREN

by Margot Early,

*available August 2007, and these other
fantastic titles from Harlequin Superromance.*

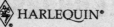

REQUEST YOUR FREE BOOKS!
2 FREE NOVELS PLUS 2
FREE GIFTS!

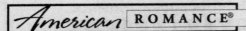

American **ROMANCE**®

Heart, Home & Happiness!

YES! Please send me 2 FREE Harlequin American Romance® novels and my 2 FREE gifts. After receiving them, if I don't wish to receive any more books, I can return the shipping statement marked "cancel." If I don't cancel, I will receive 4 brand-new novels every month and be billed just $4.24 per book in the U.S., or $4.99 per book in Canada, plus 25¢ shipping and handling per book and applicable taxes, if any*. That's a savings of close to 15% off the cover price! I understand that accepting the 2 free books and gifts places me under no obligation to buy anything. I can always return a shipment and cancel at any time. Even if I never buy another book from Harlequin, the two free books and gifts are mine to keep forever.

154 HDN EEZK   354 HDN EEZV

Name	(PLEASE PRINT)	
Address		Apt. #
City	State/Prov.	Zip/Postal Code

Signature (if under 18, a parent or guardian must sign)

Mail to the **Harlequin Reader Service**®:
IN U.S.A.: P.O. Box 1867, Buffalo, NY 14240-1867
IN CANADA: P.O. Box 609, Fort Erie, Ontario L2A 5X3

Not valid to current Harlequin American Romance subscribers.

Want to try two free books from another line?
Call 1-800-873-8635 or visit www.morefreebooks.com.

* Terms and prices subject to change without notice. NY residents add applicable sales tax. Canadian residents will be charged applicable provincial taxes and GST. This offer is limited to one order per household. All orders subject to approval. Credit or debit balances in a customer's account(s) may be offset by any other outstanding balance owed by or to the customer. Please allow 4 to 6 weeks for delivery.

Your Privacy: Harlequin is committed to protecting your privacy. Our Privacy Policy is available online at www.eHarlequin.com or upon request from the Reader Service. From time to time we make our lists of customers available to reputable firms who may have a product or service of interest to you. If you would prefer we not share your name and address, please check here. ☐

HARC

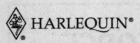

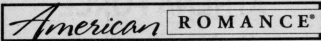

COMING NEXT MONTH

#1173 MOMMY FOR A MINUTE by Judy Christenberry
Dallas Duets

When Jack Mason came to renovate her apartment with his toddler in tow, Lauren McNabb fell for Ally—and the handsome Jack. But Jack didn't want "The Shark," as she was known in legal circles, around his child. Lauren was beautiful and, after years of being alone, kissing her felt like heaven. But could the workaholic be a mother…and a wife?

#1174 MITCH TAKES A WIFE by Ann Roth
To Wed, or Not To Wed

Fran Bishop, owner of the Oceanside B and B, has always wanted a husband and kids, but meeting men in the sleepy town of Cranberry, Oregon, isn't the easiest thing in the world. When longtime guest Mitch Matthews comes for his annual visit, Fran has no idea that their friendship is about to change—into something more permanent!

#1175 RYAN'S RENOVATION by Marin Thomas
The McKade Brothers

Brooding Ryan McKade had planned to complete his stint with a demolition company, thereby meeting his grandfather's requirement and assuring his inheritance, then be on his way. He sure as heck hadn't planned to fall for the company's secretary. Anna Nowakowski's cheery personality and trusting nature make him want to stay around longer. Except, then he'd have to reveal a few secrets—and would she still want him after he did?

#1176 GEORGIA ON HIS MIND by Ann DeFee

Win Whittaker, a top-level defense attorney from D.C., comes to Magnolia Bluffs, Georgia, on a bet. With only a hundred bucks in his pocket, he has to survive for a month. Which means he needs a job. It so happens that Kenni MacAllister's salon, Permanently Yours, has an opening for a shampoo girl. And that's how it all begins….

www.eHarlequin.com

HARCNM0707